SECRET OF THE BIG EASY

MARIE BARTEK & THE SIPS TEAM BOOK 2

ROBIN MURPHY

To my angels, who guided me to persevere and finish this novel...
thank you.

All God's angels come to us disguised.
~*James Russell Lowell*

ONE

THE SPEAKER'S voice droned on in Marie's head, and her chin slipped off the palm of her hand. She instinctively touched her throat out of habit, remembering the feel of the cord around her neck. How in the world was she going to make it through this conference if she kept falling asleep in the first seminar and replaying the nightmare of that tragedy in her head? She needed a cup of coffee, and she needed it fast.

Quietly slipping out of her chair, she headed to the back of the conference room where the catering had laid out a buffet earlier that morning. She spotted the caffeinated pot and quickly poured a cup. As she stirred the cream into her coffee, she admired the beautiful poinsettias aligning the floor around the base of the magnificent Christmas tree standing tall against the back corner of the room with an opulent golden fleur-de-lis resting at the top. The red and gold bulbs twinkled against the string of lights as the beaded gumdrop garland draped the tree in majestic contrast. Christmas was Marie's favorite holiday, and she couldn't wait to see the city decorated New Orleans style.

She felt her hip pocket vibrate, and she casually pulled her cell phone out and smiled, reading the text message from the man in her life, Cory Miller. What are you doing now? She sent a text message back saying, trying to wake up with a cup of coffee, lol. Her cell phone vibrated again. Can't wait to see you Friday. Marie replied, I'll be at the airport at 4:30 sharp, gotta go, ttyl.

Marie tucked her cell phone into her pocket and made her way back to her seat. As she tried to look interested in the speaker discussing advances and controversy in small animal endocrinology, she drifted off to the weekend plans of picking up Cory, Gale Winters, her best friend, and Tim Haines, Gale's beau, at the airport. They planned to spend the next week sightseeing in New Orleans. It was perfect timing to plan a little vacation after the National Veterinarian conference. They decided to stay at the same hotel as the conference, Le Maison de New Orleans hotel. And why not, it was the ideal spot right in the heart of the French Quarter.

The seminar broke for lunch, and Marie grabbed her materials and decided to head to her room to make some calls to her clinic. After two months of interviewing candidates, she finally hired another receptionist. It was the longest and saddest two months she ever had to endure. Trying to replace Tina Johnson was an impossible task, but Loretta Stone seemed to be fitting in well and was very organized.

Marie looked down at her name tag and read the fancy script lettering, Dr. Marie Bartek. She remembered back in June how her past came back to terrorize her, her friends, and the town of Sullivan's Island, SC. She couldn't fathom how a childhood friend could fixate on her and begin hanging women on the island. Who would have thought poor Tina Johnson would be one of the victims?

Marie was still trying to recover from that horrible hanging spree. She again woke up at night with the same recurring nightmare of the noose being wrapped around her neck and feeling the chair kick out from beneath her. It had also been a while since she had seen the spirits of the little boy and woman without a face, her guardian angels. Things had quietened down a bit. But the greatest thing to develop out of that horrible experience was having Cory in her life and organizing the Sullivan's Island Paranormal Society, SIPS. Their phones rang off the hook with people wanting investigations. There was even an article written about how they assisted in finding the serial killer in a Charleston, SC newspaper.

Marie's cell phone vibrated again, and the text message from Cory said, hate to tell you this, Bailey ate one of your shoes. Marie began to laugh and replied, which one? The returned text message read your favorite flip-flop. Marie shook her head and typed back, that's okay – I needed a new pair anyway.

Bailey was Marie's adorable chocolate Labrador retriever and a present from Cory after her recovery from a coma while in the hospital. After all of these years being a veterinarian, she never had an animal of her own. He certainly helped fill a void in her life and loved chewing on everything in sight in her beach house. She and Cory decided to let Mimi Rawlings, one of the SIPS team members, watch him while they were in New Orleans. If anyone could help train him, it would be Mimi.

Marie reached over and grabbed the phone to order room service when she felt a shocking jolt through her arm and a flash of light blinded her. She felt dizzy, and her eyes began to blur. She quickly rubbed them and realized she wasn't sitting in her room anymore. It was pitch-black, and there were images of people dressed in dark robes with hoods over their heads. Her heart began to beat to the sound of chanting that rang in her ears. She noticed the smell of sandalwood wafting in the air, which tickled her nose and made her feel listless and sleepy. Suddenly a high-pitched shriek rang out and in the middle of the group was a woman dressed in a sheer white gown trying to pull away. The images looked distorted as they danced and swooned in Marie's mind. Out of the corner of her eye, she saw a raised hand in the air holding an athame. The group moved back and there at the helm was a man wearing a ram's head. His hand struck down and stabbed the screaming woman in the heart. Before Marie could see what took place next, she was back to reality, sitting in her hotel room with the phone receiver in her hand.

Marie's shirt had become soaked clear through, and her head was pounding. She got up and went into the bathroom to splash cold water on her face. She looked at herself in the mirror and saw the dark circles under her emerald eyes. Her hands were shaking as she raked her fingers through her long golden hair. "What was that? I think I'm going to have to call Myra."

THE ROAR of the plane engines bellowed overhead while Marie waited in the short-term parking for Cory, Gale, and Tim. She drummed her fingers on the steering wheel to the beat of KT Tunstall's Black Horse and a Cherry Tree. Marie glanced in the rearview mirror and spotted Gale sashaying in front of Tim and Cory wearing a tight khaki skirt with a matching tight, bright red spandex shirt. The wedged high heel shoes she wore gave her at least five inches of added height to her already tall frame and her jet-black hair was lightly pulled back in a red silk scarf. The minute Gale spotted Marie, she began to run toward her, giving the appearance of an awkward ostrich approaching the car.

Marie got out of the car and hugged Gale. "I'm so glad to see you."

Gale kissed both of Marie's cheeks. "You and me both sistah. How are you? You look like you have dark circles under your eyes."

"That's another story. We have a lot of catching up to do." Marie felt like a dwarf next to Gale, even though she stood five foot eight.

Gale replied, "You've only been gone a week."

Marie walked over to Cory as he approached the car and kissed him hard on the lips. "You're a sight for sore eyes."

Cory cupped her chin in his hand. "Ditto, how are you doing? Have you had any more visions?"

"Visions? What visions?" Gale grabbed Marie's elbow and turned her around.

"I told you we had a lot of catching up to do."

Tim approached the opened trunk and began loading the luggage. "Why don't we continue this conversation in the car before Marie gets a ticket?" He shut the trunk. "Hi, Marie, how are you? Thanks for picking us up."

"Hello, Tim, I'm fine, and you're welcome. Aren't you, the gentleman?" Marie stuck her tongue out at Gale.

"Yeah, yeah, whatever. Come on, let's go. I'm dying to see this hotel. The pictures on the website were amazing." Gale jumped in the backseat and yanked her skirt down before it rode up to her waist.

Tim slid into the back seat next to Gale and snapped his seatbelt. "I have to say, this was a great idea." His navy baseball cap was pulled down over his brown military style haircut which gave the facade he had hair. His T-shirt clung to his swelled biceps, and his head hit the roof of the rental car. It was quite a different look than the fire chief uniform he usually wore.

Cory sat up front next to Marie. "I have always wanted to come to New Orleans. I met one of the police officers on the force here."

Marie winked. "Of course you did, and I suppose that comes with you being a police chief."

She loved the way Cory's brown curls cuddled over the tips of his ears. His mocha brown eyes matched the button-down shirt he was wearing, as his knees jammed against the front glove box.

Gale leaned forward and looked at Marie in the rearview mirror. "Okay, now what is this all about you seeing visions?"

Marie first glanced in the side view mirror and pulled out of the parking spot and then caught Gale's eyes staring back at her in the rearview mirror. "Well, it was the first day of my conference in my hotel room. I was going to order some room service when I felt this shock shoot up my arm as soon as I touched the phone receiver. There was a quick flash of light, and then the room became pitch-black."

Marie signaled to get into the passing lane and made her way onto the ramp toward the highway. "The next thing I know I'm sitting in my room, but it was as if I was in another time zone. I heard this chanting and smelled incense."

"Didn't you say something about people wearing black robes or hoods, and some woman got stabbed?" Cory took off his sunglasses.

Marie sighed. "Yeah, it looked like a satanic ritual. The woman was in this long sheer white gown, and she was screaming at the top of her lungs. Then out of nowhere, there was this figure at the head of the group wearing a ram's head."

"A what? Are you serious? Was it a real ram's head or a costume?" Gale sat back and grabbed Tim's hand.

"I couldn't tell. But the scariest thing was the man with the ram's head raising his hand in the air holding an athame. And the next thing I saw was him slamming that athame right into the screaming woman's chest. Then everything disappeared, and I was back sitting alone in my room."

"Okay, I'll ask, what's an athame?" Gale looked over at Tim's smirk. "What, you're going to tell me you know what that is?"

"As a matter of fact, I do. It's a satanic ceremonial dagger that has a double-edged blade, and it normally has a black handle. I think it's used in the Wicca religion or something." He caught Gale's surprised expression and shrugged his shoulders. "I watch a lot of science fiction shows."

Cory turned back toward Tim and Gale. "He's right. I remember reading about some occult going on a killing spree that took place in Wichita using an athame. There are a lot of psychos out there."

Marie sensed their silence and tried to make light of what they were all thinking. "And we all know about psychos, right?"

Cory chuckled and rubbed Marie's shoulder. "Yes, I think we do."

"Well, I have some interesting news. I met a gentleman at the conference by the name of André Danél. He belongs to the Big Easy Paranormal Society, BEPS for short, right here in New Orleans. He remembered seeing our photo in one of the newspapers down here and thought it might be fun to have us go along on one of their investigations." Marie blew the horn at a driver cutting her off. "What do you think? Would you all be up for that?"

"Are you kidding me? Doing an investigation in New Orleans? Hell yeah, we're up for that." Gale sat up in the seat and almost choked herself on the seat belt. "Wait, we don't have any of our equipment."

"That's okay I think we'll be able to use theirs." Marie

looked over at Cory. "Would you be interested in tagging along?"

"Sure, I think this paranormal stuff is starting to grow on me."

Gale looked out the rental car window. "We're here, look, there's the hotel. Wow, it is amazing. The balcony has a garland made of poinsettias. It looks like a palace with its grand scale and tall windows. Look at all of the Christmas lights decorating the trunks of the palm trees along the street."

"I read there were a few movies filmed here. Plus, quite a few famous authors have stayed here. I also heard it's haunted." Tim peered over Gale's shoulder.

Marie pulled into the parking lot and parked in the space marked for her room. "So, what exactly do we want to do after we check you all in? I was thinking of having dinner alfresco style. A couple of us from the conference ate right down the street at a remarkable place that served a mouthwatering chocolate torte."

"That sounds good to me. I'm starving." Tim wrestled with Gale's suitcase and almost dropped it on the ground. "What exactly did you pack for this trip? It feels like there are boulders in this thing."

"Ha, ha, very funny. It contains all of my essential needs, which you will soon be delighted I packed." Gale winked at Tim and kissed him on the cheek. "Marie, did you happen to talk to Myra about this vision?"

Myra Cummings was a psychic medium and one of the SIPS team members... and Marie's mentor. She was solely responsible for helping Marie channel her newfound psychic ability.

"Funny you should ask that, yes I did. I called her right after it happened because this never happened to me before. She called it psychometry, often referred to as object reading.

Individuals with psychometry abilities can pick up certain vibrations on an object and get a vision or feeling once they have touched the object. These vibrations are remaining energy residues from the person who owned it. Through these energy residues, a psychic can perceive information about a place, person, or event by touching an object associated with that person, place, or event. I'm obviously learning to channel my ability better, and my meditation is helping. But it still freaked me out." Marie helped carry some of Gale's luggage and headed toward the hotel lobby.

Cory grabbed Marie's hand and squeezed it hard. "I know you're pleased that you're channeling your ability more, but I get worried about all of this. Are you sleeping any better?"

Marie stopped and smiled. "A little better, I maybe only have a nightmare every other night. I'm fine. But thank you for asking."

"Hey, before I forget. I picked up your mail and left it in your dining room, but I brought along a package your mom sent." Gale wrinkled her nose at Marie's annoyed look. "I didn't open it. But can we open it soon? What did she send you?"

Marie laughed and pushed the button for the elevator. "I think it's the photos of my family ancestors. I had asked her to go through them and then send me any photos of a woman or a little boy when I came home from the hospital. She said she found quite a few in the attic from both sides of my family. We'll go through them after dinner. I want you all to try some Cajun food first."

"Aw, okay. I guess I can wait. But I need to take a quick shower." Gale squeezed her bag against Tim. "Tim, don't you need a shower, also?"

Tim smiled at Gale and kissed her nose. "Normally, I would say yes to that, but I'm starving, and we don't have any time for showering."

Gale pouted and shrugged her shoulders. "Suit yourself. But I may not be in the mood for showering later."

The elevator doors opened, and Marie shoved Gale out into the hall. "I think we get the idea of what shower means. Is half an hour enough time to freshen up?"

"Works for me, I smelled Cajun food the second we stepped out of the plane." Cory rolled his suitcase over to Marie's room and slid the card in the key slot.

"We'll be there on time. I've been dreaming about chicken gumbo." Tim stopped short at Gale's frustrated look.

"If you bring up chicken gumbo one more time, I think I'll scream." Gale opened their hotel room, rolled her suitcase inside, and let the door slam shut.

Marie looked at Tim. "What was that all about?"

Cory answered first. "Let's just say Tim obviously likes chicken gumbo and repeatedly reminded us of it during the entire flight."

Tim shrugged his shoulders and knocked lightly on the door. "Gale, please let me in. I don't have the keycard." The door opened for a split second and Tim slipped through before it closed on him.

Marie started to laugh and followed Cory into their room. "I guess we don't have any time for a shower, either."

Cory pulled Marie into his arms. "Oh, I think we have plenty of time. I'm not as hungry as Tim."

Marie giggled and propped her chin on Cory's chest. "I like the way you think, Chief Miller."

TWO

MARIE LOVED how the streets in the French Quarter were aligned in an orderly grid, which encompassed brick and cobblestone sidewalks with historical buildings sandwiched together. Each business sat neatly tucked beneath a wrought iron balcony displaying their wares or menu items. Christmas certainly came alive everywhere with the lights, red velvet bows, ornaments, and wreaths.

The restaurant they chose boasted of Cajun cuisine and French ambiance with aged rustic brown brick walls and wide planked wooden doors that welcomed everyone inside, as well as outside at the alfresco café. The red-ribbon lined garland was strung around the wrought iron gas light fixtures, which harmonized with the table and chairs along the sidewalk. The distant sound of zydeco music echoed throughout the street. It gave one a sense of class in a relaxed atmosphere.

They finished their meals of chicken gumbo, crawfish cakes, shrimp, and turtle soup. A traditional dinner wouldn't be complete without New Orleans cocktail of choice, Sazerac, which is the famed mix of rye whiskey, bitters, and absinthe that originated in the bayou. The finale to the meal was bananas foster with vanilla ice cream, and fresh ground coffee.

Gale sat back in her chair and held her hand to her stomach. "That had to be one of the best meals I have ever eaten. I would need to work out after every meal if I lived here."

Marie smiled and sipped her coffee. "I know, right? I refuse to use the scale when I get home."

"I'm only going to say this one last time, but that was the best chicken gumbo ever." Tim awkwardly looked at Gale and Cory. "I promise never to mention it again."

Cory laughed and placed his napkin on the table. "After that meal, you can say chicken gumbo anytime you want. I wasn't sure how I was going to like the crawfish cakes, but they were delicious."

"Marie, tell me more about this psycho chemistry stuff Myra was telling you about. When did you start having the ability to see things when you touched them?" Gale leaned toward Tim and wiped a smudge of ice cream off his chin with her napkin.

"Its *psychometry* and that was the first time it ever happened. It was so surreal. I could feel the fear from the woman who was stabbed and the eeriness throughout the whole vision. The incense made me feel drugged. My shirt was soaked clear through when I came back around."

Gale gave Marie a concerned look. "I think I have to agree with Cory, I'm glad you're getting a handle on all of this, but it almost feels as though you're getting deeper into new abilities. Was Myra concerned?"

Marie smiled, thinking of Myra and her tiny, frail frame wearing her brightly colored wardrobe and flashy jewelry. Even though Myra was only in her sixties, she looked antiquated.

"A little at first, but she helped me through it. I asked her if the vision could have taken place in my hotel room. She said it was possible, or that whoever stayed in that room took part in the ritual someplace else. She also said it could have happened at any time and that the energy residues remained on the phone. Or something like that, it was all a bit confusing to me."

"Yeah, I bet. We may need to stay in touch with her this week if it happens again." Gale tucked her hair behind her ear.

Tim sat up in his chair. "What do you all say we get the real feel of New Orleans and walk the streets of the French Quarter? Maybe we can check out some voodoo shops."

"Ooh, yeah, and I'd love to see if there are any antique shops around with the off chance of taking something back to my shop." Gale rubbed her hands together.

Gale owned the local antique shop on Sullivan's Island and only lived three beach houses up from Marie, which was a nice bonus when Marie was itching to buy antiques for her home or clinic.

Marie stood up and stretched her back. "I think that's a great idea. I need to walk off this meal. Let's head down Dauphine Street, and maybe we can catch a trolley."

They made their way and caught a trolley that was painted bright red with yellow folding doors adorned with Christmas lights. There was fake snow on the roof and the tall windows wrapped around the entire trolley giving them the ability to see the spectacular views and decorations along the streets. You could hear the metal trolley pole slide across the overhead wire, while the steel wheels ground along on the rails and the sound of the trolley bell echoed throughout the car and streets.

After frequenting many points of interest, Marie waited for everyone outside one of the voodoo shops. "These shops are touristy but fun."

Gale pouted and stepped down onto the brick sidewalk. "Why wouldn't you let me buy one of those voodoo dolls?"

Marie rolled her eyes. "Because you wanted it to look like Harry."

Harry Connor was a school counselor and demonologist, and one of the SIPS team members.

"Those aren't to be taken lightly. Just like Ouija boards. They're sold as casual games, but I don't like tempting fate." Marie elbowed Gale to make her laugh.

Cory pulled out his New Orleans street map. "Hey, we're only a block away from the St. Louis Cemetery, anyone in the mood to take a tour?"

Gale quickly stopped pouting. "Yeah, let's see if they're giving any ghost tours."

"Really? You want to take a ghost tour when you're a member of a ghost investigation team?" Tim chuckled and shook his head.

"Well yeah, why not? You said we should get the full experience of New Orleans."

Marie smiled at Gale and shrugged her shoulders. "I'm game if any of you are?"

Tim glanced down at his watch. "Do you think any tours are going on now? I mean it's almost eleven o'clock."

"There's only one way to find out. Let's head over there." Cory folded the map and slipped it into his back pants pocket.

Marie arrived first at the signboard posted on the concrete pillars and read the times for cemetery tours. "It looks as though we will have to come back in the morning. Their tours are at ten, and it closed at three."

"Hey, the gates are open. So is the lock." Gale cautiously walked through the tall iron gate.

The cemetery at night was imposing and eerie. Every tomb sat above ground and gave the appearance the bodies would leap out at you. The statues of saints cast their shadowy figures against the mausoleums making you feel as though you were being watched. Some tombs were quite dull and decrepit, while others were covered with flowers and mementos.

"Wow, it's claustrophobic in here. How can anyone pack all of these bodies in such a small space?" Gale edged up against a mausoleum. "Isn't the grave of that voodoo queen in here?"

"Marie Laveau, and yes I think it is. Or it's her daughter's grave. I can't remember offhand." Tim followed Gale and grabbed her hand.

"Okay, I'm not even going to ask how you know that. What do you do, sit up at two in the morning and watch all the freak shows on TV?" Gale chuckled and laced her arm in his.

Cory laughed. "What else has he got to do when he's pulling the night shift at the fire station?"

Marie smiled and gazed around the cemetery. "I have to say, this would be a great place for an investigation."

"Speaking of which, this André Danél you met, did he happen to say what they were going to be investigating? And when are we going to meet him?" Gale stopped short at a majestic monument of an angel towering over them.

"He's going to give me a call tomorrow. I think he mentioned about us attending their meeting in the evening. That'll give us the chance to meet the rest of the team." Marie felt a cold chill and shivered. "As far as what the investigation is, we'll have to wait and see."

Cory rubbed Marie's shoulders. "Are you okay? Do you want my jacket?"

"No, I'm fine, I just felt a chill." Marie continued walking and suddenly felt dizzy. "Whoa, my head is spinning. And I feel a little clammy."

Cory grabbed Marie's arm and guided her to a grave with crumbling bricks. "I think you'd better sit down over here."

Gale handed Marie her bottle of water. "Are you having one of those visions?"

"I think I am. I can see a woman in a sheer nightgown. Or at least I think she's in a nightgown." Marie rubbed her temples and closed her eyes. "Wait a minute, she's saying something. She's holding her chest, and there's blood. Oh wow, there's blood all over her chest."

Marie's voice trailed off, and she felt herself slipping into a dreamlike state. The woman in the nightgown was screaming and holding her hands out to Marie. Images of people flashed by in a haze, and there were voices of chanting and loud drumming. They appeared to be dancing a strange dance around a fire. Suddenly there was a woman in the middle holding a snake that coiled its slithering body around her neck. The woman's eyes were glowing, and she stared at Marie with such intensity that she could feel a sharp pain in her chest. Marie's throat began to feel dry, and she started to gag. She couldn't catch her breath. She felt as if she would choke to death when her guardian angels appeared in a glowing halo. They were calling out to Marie and pulling her away from the fire. There were bright colors of yellow and gold, and Marie felt as if she was in the middle of a typhoon. She kept slipping and spinning and falling until everything was still and dark.

Marie opened her eyes and found herself staring up at a woman with copper-colored skin and deep bronze eyes. "Where am I? What happened?"

"Ya were havin' a vision chile. But ya were slippin' too far into it. I brought ya back to da present." The woman slowly lifted Marie's head and leaned her against Cory. "My name is Delia Boisseau. I am a psychic reader at the voodoo museum. Ya spirit guides brought me to ya."

Marie slowly sat up and saw everyone staring at her with pale faces. "Spirit guides? What spirit guides?"

Delia asked, "Baby, don't ya know what a spirit guide is?"

"No, I'm afraid I don't. I'm a little new to this."

"A spirit guide is like ya guardian angels. Do ya know what dose are?" Delia smiled and stood up wearing a traditional koto dress with bright orange and yellow flowers and an angisa head wrap to match.

"Yes, yes I do. I did see them." She turned to Cory and the others. "I saw the little boy and woman without a face again. In fact, just as I saw them everything went bright and gold. Then it went pitch-dark, and I woke up."

"Dat's right. They summoned me to bring ya back from da vision. Ya was too far gone, and they was protecting ya." Delia leaned forward and placed her hand on Marie's head and closed her eyes. "Chile you have a whole lotta things rollin' around in dat head of yas."

Gale stepped forward and smiled at Delia. "Thank you for helping my friend. She just recently got a handle on having her ability to talk with spirits about six months ago. And now there seems to be more she's able to do."

"Don't y'all fret. The spirit guides will protect her. And I'll be around too." Her smile faded as she looked back at Marie. "But I is here to tell ya dat ya need to be careful with dat vision. Y'all be messin' with voodoo and da occult. Close ya mind chile. When they be tryin' to get into ya head, tell dem to back away. They is powerful."

"I will. I'll do the best I can. And thank you for your help." Marie extended her hand to Delia.

Delia shook her hand and smiled. "Dat's all ya can do. Now y'all best head on outta here before da police see ya in here and I best be gettin' back to da museum. If y'all have any more questions, stop on by."

They all smiled and waved good bye as she sashayed out through the iron gates and disappeared around the corner.

Cory helped Marie to her feet. "I think that was enough for one evening, don't you?"

"Yeah, I have to say, I'm not so sure I want to have a tour of this place now." Tim grabbed Gale's hand.

"Marie, why don't we head back to the hotel and maybe call Myra in the morning. I think we need to keep her in the loop of what just happened. She may have some insight on it." Gale linked her arm with Marie's.

"Yeah, I agree. I also think I'm going to need to work on my meditation. I need to be able to control my mind when the spirits are trying to communicate with me. It was just so over-powering." Marie leaned her head on Cory's shoulder.

"I'm not prepared to go through that again. My heart dropped out of my chest when you weren't responding." Cory kissed Marie's forehead.

"I know, right? Then all of a sudden out of nowhere, Madam Delia shows up snapping her fingers in front of your face and chanting some voodoo language all over you. That was freaky." Gale shook her head and shivered.

Tim draped his arm around Gale. "I hear ya, but I think it was Creole she was speaking."

"Okay, I need to monitor your television programs. You're starting to scare me." Gale giggled and poked Tim's side.

Marie sighed. "I'm exhausted. It completely drained me."

Gale stopped walking and turned to Marie. "What exactly was the vision anyway?"

"From what I could make of it, some voodoo ceremony around a fire with a voodoo priestess dancing with a snake around her shoulders. She stared right at me with glowing green eyes. Oh, and that same woman I saw in my hotel room was there screaming and holding out her hands to me. What's that all about?" Marie took another sip of Gale's bottled water.

Cory guided Marie to continue walking. "I definitely think you need to talk to Myra and get a good night's rest. I'm exhausted just by listening to all of this."

They all walked arm in arm back to their hotel. Marie felt woozy and weary from the whole experience. There was no doubt this latest vision scared her. But she was glad to see her spirit guides or guardian angels again. It was nice to know she had good friends here and on the other side protecting her.

THREE

THE CONTINUOUS PLAYBACK of the voodoo priestess' glowing green eyes, and loud rhythmic drumming, brought on a restless night of sleep for Marie. She decided to take a quick shower and go through the package of pictures her mother sent. Her stomach growled as she started the small coffee pot in their room.

Quietly opening the box, she heard footsteps behind her and, she turned and smiled. "Good morning. I was trying to stay as quiet as possible. Sorry if I woke you."

"You didn't wake me, the coffee did." Cory sat down on the floor next to Marie. "Besides, it's very lonely when you're not in bed with me."

Marie grinned. "I'm beginning to grow on you, aren't I? Even with all of my special abilities? I can't believe you're still around."

Cory brushed a strand of hair back from her face and tucked it behind her ear. "Oh, I think it's going to take a whole lot more to scare me off. I thought you were going to wait for Gale to go through these pictures."

"I know, but I couldn't sleep, and it's been bugging me to check these out. She'll forgive me... I hope."

Cory helped spread the pictures out on the floor and turned a photo around and read the back. "Your mom sure is organized. She has the names and dates written on every one of these."

"Yes, that's my mom, organized." Marie spotted a photo of a woman and immediately picked it up. "This is her. This is the woman without a face... my spirit guide."

She flipped the photo over and read. "Ladislava Maria Hynick. Cory, this is her. This is the woman who is my guardian angel. Hynick is the last name of my grandmother on my father's side. It says here she is my fourth great grandmother. Wow, I can't believe it. I wonder why she never seems to reveal her face to me in my visions. But when I was in my coma, I was able to see her face."

"This is way out of my league. Maybe when you call Myra, she'll be able to shed some light on it."

Marie jumped at the knock on the door. "I bet that's Gale and Tim. Would you mind letting them in?"

Cory opened the door. "Good morning, Gale, come on in. Where's Tim?"

"Oh, he's mesmerized with the tugboats going up and down the Mississippi. He's been staring out of our hotel room window all morning." Gale looked at Marie and placed her laptop on the counter. "Hey, you were supposed to wait for me to go through those pictures, remember?"

"I know, I know, but I couldn't sleep." Marie held up the picture of her ancestor. "Look, this is her, my spirit guide. This is my fourth great grandmother. Can you believe it?"

Gale took the photo and read the back. "Wow, what a name. What is this Polish?"

"No, I think it's Slovak. Her middle name is close to mine."

Tim entered the room before the door closed and glanced at the photo. "She looks just like you described her... without the face, that is."

Cory sat back down next to Marie and handed her a cup of coffee. "Have you found the picture of the little boy?"

"No, not yet. But there's more in the box."

Gale sat down and moved the laptop on the floor. "Look, I called Myra this morning, and she's at the ready with the team at your place so we can Skype. I thought that would be the best way to communicate with everyone. What do you think?"

"I think that's perfect. Thank you." Marie took a sip of coffee. "How did Myra sound?"

"She was worried. She wishes she could be here to help you. Especially after I told her what happened in the cemetery." Gale logged onto her account and waited for Mimi to answer.

Tim sat behind Gale. "What are we doing for breakfast? Should we order room service?"

"I think that'll be easier. Why don't I order some things off the menu while you're Skyping?" Cory got up and grabbed the menu next to the phone.

"Works for me, I'm starving." Marie shuffled through more pictures and stopped dead in her tracks. "Oh my gosh, this is him. This is the little boy spirit guide. I can't believe this."

Gale took the picture and flipped it over. "It says here the name is Ludomir Zoran Courty. What kind of a name is that?"

Marie took the photo back and stared at the face. "I don't know, but I think I remember that name from somewhere. I think it may be French. It doesn't say how we're related."

The laptop rang, and Mimi's plump face appeared along with Bailey licking the keyboard. "Good morning. We're all here."

Marie put the photo down and moved toward the laptop

and smiled. "Hey good morning everyone, thanks so much for getting up to do this. Hello Bailey, how's my good boy? How many flip-flops have you eaten?"

Mimi picked up Bailey and set him on the floor. "I haven't seen any eaten flip-flops, but he tried chewing on the leg of your walnut dining table. I caught him in time."

Marie shook her head and laughed. "Thanks, Mimi, I so appreciate you watching over him. I can't wait to get back home. I miss his wake-up licks in the morning. Hey, where's Myra?"

"I'm right here, dear. How are you?" Myra was wearing a purple sweater over a wild green paisley shirt. Her earrings danced from her ears against her shoulders.

"I'm fine, a little frazzled. So, you heard the details of my encounter yesterday?" Marie rolled over onto her stomach.

"Yes, Gale explained to me what you witnessed. Why don't you explain to me exactly what you saw and felt? This will help me to get a handle a little better as to what happened to you."

Marie explained in precise detail the vision she had in the cemetery describing the smells, colors, spirits, and voodoo dance. When she was finished, the group began discussing their theories.

"I have to say that was a crazy vision, Marie. I'm glad you're okay." Jim Rawlings rubbed his chin and shook his head. His thin face looked pale, and his receding hairline continued to disappear up his forehead. One would guess that was due to being married to Mimi.

"I'm not quite sure how I would have handled that." Mimi leaned in toward their laptop to reveal her double chin. Her salt and pepper hair was tightly curled, and her reading glasses hung from a gold chain around her neck.

Harry Connor wiped his forehead with a greasy looking handkerchief and bumped his glasses, which revealed new tape on the sides. The black and white herringbone bow tie clashed with his brown tweed suit. "I'd like to do a little more research on voodoo and the occult. I do believe you'd better not delve too deeply into it."

"Oh, trust me. I plan on taking this very slowly." Marie shifted onto her right elbow. "Myra, what do you make of these visions? Why did I see the same woman in both the occult ritual and voodoo dance?"

Myra sighed and leaned her head to the left. "I believe this woman you are seeing is sharing memories with you. Spirits do that to help you better understand what happened and how they feel. I think you need to check with the authorities to see if anyone was murdered in a sinister way. Or check the missing persons. For this woman to have appeared to you twice, I believe she's trying to send you an urgent message, dear."

"I tend to agree. Is there anyone there who you can contact?" Harry tried to peer around Mimi's head.

"Well yeah, Cory said he knows someone on the police force here." Marie turned toward Cory. "Who was it you said you knew?"

"His name's Jesse Irons. He was a guest lecturer at the Federal Law Enforcement Training Center during my training. I haven't talked to him since then. I guess I could look him up and see if he's still with the department here." Cory set the menu down on the table. "Let me get the phonebook and look up the number."

"Marie, Gale explained to me that your guardian angels guided Ms. Boisseau to help you to come back out of your vision." Myra's smile waned. "I'm a little concerned that you were pulled that deeply into the vision to warrant help to bring you out of it. Dear, have you been practicing your meditation?"

Marie smiled. "I knew you were going to ask me that. Yes, I have, but not well enough. Myra, this was unbelievably strong.

I lost all control of my mind and body. Every time I tried to pull away and bring myself back, I felt myself being sucked back in."

"Remember to use the azurite crystals I gave to you, do you have them with you?"

"Yes, I do. But I did forget to put the crystals under my pillow. Oh, and I need to remember to wear the one around my neck." Marie sat up in a yoga position. "Do you think those will help?"

Myra nodded. "Absolutely dear, and you must also remember how to manage and direct the energy with your thoughts and intentions through the law of attraction. That will help you to pull yourself out of a negative vision. Ms. Boisseau was correct in telling you to stay away from the occult. It can be a scary and deeply evil religion if it's misused."

Gale shifted toward the laptop. "Wait a minute. I didn't tell you anything about what Madam Delia said about the occult. How did you know that?"

Myra grinned. "Ah, yes, well, don't you think we were all trying to help pull Marie out of that vision?"

Marie's forehead shot straight up. "You mean to tell me you already knew about this vision? Wait, what am I asking that for? Of course, you did."

"Your guardian angels, or as Ms. Boisseau stated, your spirit guides, summoned me also dear. You must always remember that I, too, am always with you." Myra affectionately smiled.

Cory hung up his cell phone and sat down next to Marie. "Well, I was able to get a hold of Jesse. I found out he's no longer just a detective on the force, but the commander of the Offense against Persons Division within the Investigation and Support Bureau, meaning the homicide division. He's moved up. I carefully tried to explain to him about your vision. I'm not sure if he's buying any of it. But having lived here all of his life, he knows about psychics. He did get reticent when I gave him the details of the woman in the sheer nightgown in the satanic ritual in Marie's vision. He asked me to have her come down tomorrow morning to meet with their sketch artist. He wouldn't elaborate on anything, but he said there had been a cold case he's been working on that is similar to her vision."

Gale shivered. "Wow, I just got goosebumps on my arm."

"That works for me. I want to get to the bottom of this." Marie looked back at the team. "We were invited to do an investigation with the Big Easy Paranormal Society sometime this week. I'm expecting a call from one of the cofounders today. As soon as we receive the details, I'd like to keep you all in the loop. I'm sorry we couldn't have you all down here."

Jim shrugged. "That's okay. We can communicate well enough."

Marie smiled. "Someone is knocking at our door. It looks like our breakfast has arrived. Thanks again for all of your insight. Myra, I thank you, as always, for having my back. I promise to keep the crystals close and to practice meditating more. I may need you to stay on call for me."

"Of course, dear, I'll be here any time of the day or night. Let us know what you find out at the police department."

"Bye, everyone, we'll stay in touch." Gale logged off and shut her laptop.

Tim wheeled the breakfast cart into the room. "Wow, this looks delicious. Take a look at all of these beignets and omelets."

Gale looked at Tim. "What is a beignet?"

"It's like a fritter. They're loaded with powdered sugar." Tim took a bite of a beignet and plastered powdered sugar all over his face.

Gale asked, "And you know this how?"

"I did a little research on New Orleans cuisine before we

came. I like to know the history of a place." Tim wiped the sugar off of his face and smeared it across his cheek.

Gale handed Tim a napkin. "I'm having a hard time taking you seriously with powdered sugar all over your face."

Marie grabbed a plate and plopped an omelet topped with chili and fries. "Wow, I have to say I haven't seen this combination before."

"I think after we eat, we should try and get in touch with André and find out where we need to meet them this evening." Cory poured orange juice and took a bite of bacon.

"I agree. I have his number in my wallet. I think their headquarters are in the French Quarter somewhere."

Gale tried to speak without spitting powdered sugar everywhere. "I think we should go over to the historic voodoo museum and have a chat with Madam Boisseau. Don't you think we need to learn more about what happened last evening? Maybe she can help you on all of this."

"Let me give André a call and organize where and when to meet them. We can walk over to the museum after breakfast." Marie set down her fork and pulled out her cell phone to make the call.

FOUR

Marie stood in front of the Napoleon House and stared up at the top floor. The building was the central connecting point of two streets while its roof leaned upon simple wooden posts and displayed faded peeling stucco walls. It seemed humorous to see Christmas lights strung around the windows twinkling on and off in sequence.

"Well, this is it. André said to meet him up on the third floor." Marie peeked through the window of the hunter green painted double doors.

Tim stuck his nose in the air and sniffed. "This is someplace. I can smell the food way out here."

Gale laughed. "Let me guess, you want more chicken gumbo."

Cory opened the door for everyone. "We just had dinner an hour ago. How could he want more chicken gumbo?"

They all chuckled and walked into the main entrance of the restaurant and immediately smelled the aroma of peppers and onions with hints of cayenne pepper and garlic being stirred around from the overhead ceiling fans. The noise of conversations and laughter rang throughout the bar with the clinking of glasses and silverware hitting the china plates.

Cory pointed to the back stairway. "I think that's where we need to go. I see the exit sign André told you about."

"Yep, that's it." Marie pointed to the walls. "Check out the cool pictures."

Gale's jaw dropped as she gazed at a patron's plate of food. "Check out the size of that sandwich. Man, we need to come back here for dinner and some beer."

Tim prodded Gale's back to hurry her along. "Count me in."

They reached the top of the stairs and heard voices in the distance coming from the end of the hall. There was a light emanating from a doorway casting a feathered shadow of smoke.

Marie approached first and lightly rapped on the door jamb. "Hello, is this the Big Easy Paranormal Society meeting?"

André looked up and smiled. "Marie, please come in. I see you found us. Let me introduce you to everyone." His salt and pepper hair matched his close-shaven beard, and his eyes were the color of lightly creamed coffee.

Cory, Gale, and Tim followed Marie into the room and began shaking hands with the members of BEPS. They met Katherine Martin, who was petite with short cropped black hair and tiny narrow eyes. She was a native N'awliner and owned an art studio on Canal Street. Jason Blanc was a huge, rounded man with balding grey hair and the owner of Napoleon House. It was apparent the smoke they saw in the hall was coming from his cigar, which hung out the side of his mouth. Philippe Lacoste was a French Creole attorney. He was tall and distinguished with a thin finely groomed carbon mustache. At the other end of the table sat Brigitte Dubois, a bartender, who wore a low-cut blouse and bright red lipstick.

Her smoldering blue eyes and flaxen blonde hair stole Tim's attention, causing Gale to remind him to keep his eyes front and center.

"We certainly welcome the members from the SIPS team here tonight. We're excited to include you in our investigation of the LaLaurie House. It's considered to be one of the most haunted places here in New Orleans." André turned toward the wall and pulled down a projector screen. "Katherine, would you please turn off the lights for us?"

Katherine obliged and sat back down next to Jason. "Be sure to exit out of the email account before you begin using the power point presentation."

"Thank you for the reminder, Katherine." André smiled and looked at Marie. "I'm not very tech savvy."

Jason gruffly chuckled. "No, you shouldn't be using computers at all."

"Okay, let's continue with the history of this grand house." André tapped the enter key on the computer. "As you can see this photo of the LaLaurie House was taken sometime in the 1830s and was the same time Delphine LaLaurie and her third husband, Leonard, took up residence there. They were considered to be the sweethearts of the New Orleans social scene. Madame LaLaurie hosted amazing events at her home, which were talked about months after."

"She is considered to be sweet and endearin', and her husband is very well respected within the community." Brigitte smiled and winked at André.

"Yes, they were. Madame LaLaurie also befriended the infamous Voodoo Queen, Marie Laveau. Marie didn't live far from their home on Royal Street, and they became more acquainted as Marie Laveau occasionally did Delphine's hair." André looked back at the group. "And eventually under Marie's tutelage, Delphine began to act on her hidden interest in the occult and began learning the secrets of voodoo."

"Now, like all well-established members of society, the LaLaurie's owned slaves to run their home on Royal Street. There wasn't anything unusual about Madame LaLaurie and her slaves, although some said they held her in nervous regard." André flipped to the next picture of Delphine LaLaurie. "As time went on there were whispers amongst the slaves and the free people of color of the abuse of LaLaurie's slaves. But the socialites turned a deaf ear to the rumors until the day Madame LaLaurie was seen chasing a slave girl through the house and to her ultimate death three stories below on the cobblestone courtyard."

"It was deemed an accident, and the LaLaurie's felt they were perfectly within their rights to enact such discipline on the slaves. How very tris." Philippe shook his head.

"Yes, and one of the women slaves from the kitchen was infuriated with the events that took place in the house, so she decided to light a fire which had engulfed most of the lower stories. When the fire brigade arrived, she claimed there were poor souls in the attic. There were witnessed accounts of dead and half-dead slaves of men, women, and children found in the attic." Katherine paused and shifted in her seat. "They were chained to the walls by shackles on their hands and feet, and they had been subjected to unimaginable acts of morbid atrocity: eyes gouged out; tongues hacked off, and in some instances, crudely reattached; mouths and eyes sewn shut altogether; noses and ears sheared off; bones broken and reset in horrible, twisted manners; and genitals mutilated. These were just some of the horrible sights that met the eyes of the fire rescuers and witnessed by ordinary citizens."

Gale's mouth dropped open and quickly closed. "That's just plain, repulsive."

André continued. "Yes, well, the city was in an uproar and wanted revenge. Many said that Madame LaLaurie escaped and took refuge and continued this practice in France, while others said she escaped to the North shore woods where her anger festered over the years along with her interest in the dark learned at the hand of Marie Laveau."

Jason puffed on his cigar while smoke edged out of the side of his mouth. "The house was renovated many times over. Families have lived there. I think it was a school and a clothing shop once. Now it's been turned into a bunch of studios and apartments."

Katherine leaned forward on the table. "Reports have indicated the sounds of moaning and weeping supposedly from the tortured souls in the attic. People have heard running, slamming doors, and shouts from the spirits who remain going on about their business. Some have even said they saw Madame LaLaurie herself. More tales surface every day with new occurrences."

André turned off the computer. "Can someone please turn on the lights? As you can see, there is quite a bit of activity going on in the LaLaurie House. We had our preliminary walk-through last week to be sure of where we need to set up our equipment. We'll make sure we fill you in on where the obstacles are. We are scheduled to do the investigation this Tuesday. We are excited to have you as our guests."

Marie smiled. "Thank you, André, and thank you all for allowing us to be your guests. I think we're pretty excited about it as well."

André turned to his team. "Does anyone have any questions?"

"Yeah, I do." Brigitte leaned forward, revealing quite a bit of cleavage. "How long have y'all been investigating as a team?

André mentioned y'all helped solve a case involving a serial killer that was plaguing your island."

Marie smiled. "Yes, that's somewhat true, and we've been investigating together for about six months." She glanced over at Cory and proceeded after his approving nod. "I'm not sure what information André filled you in on, but I have the ability to see and talk to spirits. I've had this ability since I was twelve but squelched it for the last eighteen years. Up until about six or seven months ago, my ability began to come back to me in full force. Along with me learning to channel that ability with the help of one of our team members and my very dear friend and mentor, a serial killer began a killing spree on the women in and around Sullivan's Island."

"I remember reading the article André brought to one of our meetings. This killer was an old friend of yours?" Jason blew smoke right into Gale's face and ignored her muffled cough.

"Yes, you are correct. He, Davey McGee, was a childhood friend, but I hadn't spoken to him since I was twelve. He began to follow me, without my knowledge, and became obsessed with my life." Marie stood up and began to pace around the room, gaining confidence to continue with the nightmare she had been dealing with over the last six months. "You see, his mother hung herself after years of physical and emotional abuse from her husband, Davey's father. Davey knew I could speak to spirits and begged me to talk with his mother. He never knew the abuse his father did to his mother. And when I told him the truth, he screamed and yelled and called me a liar and a fraud which prompted me to squelch my ability. I guess he pretty much went nuts and planned his revenge on me."

"The article stated he hung you and it put you into a coma." Philippe ran his thumb and forefinger over his mustache.

"Yes, he did... and it did. I still have nightmares from it. But it's easing a bit." Marie sat back down next to Cory and met his hand under the table.

"How were you able to help with the case?" Katherine closed the laptop and put it away.

Cory replied, "Marie admitted to me she could see and hear spirits. Being a police chief and trained to solve cases with facts, I was a bit skeptical at first, but all of the visions she had relating to the case were too coincidental. Between Marie and Myra, their other psychic medium, and the team here, we were able to catch him just in time."

"Wow, aren't you a bit young to be police chief?" Brigitte leaned back in her chair.

Cory smiled. "They were having a hard time finding someone to take the position for the amount of pay... small town and all."

André smiled. "We're glad you can help us out on Tuesday. If that's all for the questions, how about we invite the SIPS team with us to our usual place for some great music?"

"That sounds perfect to me." Brigitte looked at Tim. "Would y'all be in the mood for some belly rubbin' music?"

Gale smiled wide and pulled Tim against her. "Oh, I think that would be wonderful. Tim and I just love to belly rub."

"Great, then why don't we all head down to Preservation Hall? I know the owner, so you won't need to worry about the cover charge." André grabbed the laptop and followed the group toward the door. "Get ready for close quarters as there are only benches to sit on. But once the music starts, the frills won't matter."

They arrived at Preservation Hall within minutes and gazed upon a building that looked as if it had been abandoned. Passersby shunned the sad look of faded painted stucco and worn wooden shutters. They walked to the side of the building and admired the lovely old music posters of days gone past hanging on the walls. If it weren't for the sound of the music escaping from the inside, they would have ignored entering through the rusted wrought iron gates altogether.

Marie peered up into the tiny room and felt as if she had stepped back in time. She could barely see the pale white-washed milk paint beneath the scores of crookedly hung pictures, signs, and tack board. The film of dirt layered around the windows and doors was an inch thick. But it was nice to see the attempt made to create Christmas cheer through plastic potted poinsettias and wreaths displayed behind the musicians.

The Preservation Hall Jazz Band was already in full swing, and the place was packed. There were people sitting tightly against each other on benches along the wall and cushions on the floor. Heads bounced and swayed as others clapped, allowing their shoulders to dance with the music.

"We can stand against the wall over there." André pointed to the back of the room. "Go ahead and follow Brigitte. She knows where to go."

Gale whispered in Marie's ear. "I bet she does."

Marie rolled her eyes and nudged Gale to keep moving. "I'm sensing some tension in the air."

Cory leaned over and yelled into Marie's ear. "That guy sounds just like Louis Armstrong."

"I know he's amazing." Marie smiled and bobbed her head while leaning against the wall.

Tim tried to talk over the music. "They only have five members playing, but you'd think there were more."

André leaned over toward Marie. "I understand you had a vision in the cemetery last evening."

Marie gave a shocked look and nodded. "Yes, I did, but how did you find out about it?"

André laughed. "It's a small town here in New Orleans,

especially around the French Quarter. Delia Boisseau is a very dear friend of mine. She's an amazing psychic medium. I've known her since I was a young boy. She and my mother were best friends."

"Were? What happened?"

"My mother died of lung cancer when I was twenty. Delia knew before my mother did that she was going to go to the other side, home as she called it. My mother made Delia promise not to tell me, and I'm grateful. One should never give up on hope. Delia has shared with me that my mother visits often and is always around protecting me, which I find to be very comforting."

Marie shook her head. "I'm so sorry to hear that your mother passed. I lost an aunt to breast cancer. It's always intrigued me how people who cross over to the other side can still be around you."

"Delia has explained that spirits are ones who have gone home and will come back to help you during difficult times in life, or when they sense you may be in danger. Ghosts, on the other hand, are considered to be trapped between our world and the other side. Most of the time, they don't even realize they're dead. Or they're too afraid to cross over thinking that their previous life wasn't worthy of them to cross." André clapped with the crowd when the song was over. "You see, from what I have learned, spirits live in another dimension that is only about three feet above earth's ground level. And they live at a much higher vibrational frequency than we do, which is why we don't recognize our proximity to it. An example would be why the human ear can't hear the high-frequency pitch of a dog whistle. If you've ever heard of someone who has had an experience with seeing a spirit, their descriptions have always included the spirits are floating about three feet off the ground."

"That's what my spirit guides do." Marie stopped short and stared at André.

"That's okay. I know about spirit guides. I have one too. We all do." André turned toward Marie and leaned his shoulder against the wall. "You see, that's the difference between seeing a spirit and a ghost. A ghost never appears to be floating; they're trapped in the ghost dimension. The best analogy I can use to differentiate between all three dimensions is to picture the spokes in the wheel of a bicycle. Visualize the slowest speed of the wheel where the spokes are easy to see, that would be earth's dimension, you and me. At medium speed, the spokes begin to blur and are harder for our eyes to see, that would represent the dimension of the ghost. Then at the highest speed of the wheel where the spokes look as if they don't exist at all would be the dimension of a spirit."

"That makes sense. When my spirit guides have appeared to me, they appeared to be floating, whereas the ghost of the woman that has come to me in these latest visions isn't." Marie stood away from the wall and rubbed her back.

"Exactly, it's hard to explain to people. They tend to look at you as if you're crazy." André looked at his watch. "Wow, we've been standing here talking for over an hour. They close at eleven. We can continue this conversation tomorrow if you like?"

"That would be great, maybe after lunch some time. I'm meeting a Commander Irons at the police department tomorrow with Cory. Commander Irons was intrigued with my vision. Apparently, it matches up with a cold case."

"Ah, yes, I know Commander Irons, he's a good guy. I also seem to remember hearing about a girl being murdered with an athame, and it was leaning toward a lot of voodoo and satanic cult rituals."

"Wow, you do hear all of the gossip, don't you?" Marie saw the team beginning to meander toward the door.

"Well yes, and Delia filled me in on your visions. I think you should sit down with her some time as well. Maybe I can organize getting together with her and your team over dinner. Would you all be up for that?" André motioned to his team to leave.

"Yes, that would be great. We wanted to go and see Delia earlier today, but we never got around to it. I think she would be accommodating in all of this. I still need some guidance on this whole ability of mine."

Gale leaned closer to Marie to hear the conversation. "Oh, good. I wanted to go back and talk to her."

André replied, "Great, that sounds like a plan. I have your cell phone number, and I'll give you a call after I talk with Delia. Maybe you'll have more details after you meet with Commander Irons."

The two teams said their goodbyes and agreed to meet for dinner the next day with Delia. As they headed back to their hotel, Marie filled everybody in on the explanation André gave about the difference between spirits and ghosts. They all felt it was interesting information, but Marie still wondered how all of this tied in with the woman ghost who insisted on sharing her misfortune through finite detail, and what her meeting with the sketch artist would reveal.

FIVE

MARIE SQUINTED at the sketch and tilted her head. "Yes, I think that's it. That looks exactly like the woman I saw in my vision at the hotel and the cemetery."

The sketch artist made some final touches with his pencil. His crimson hair stuck up high and stiff through the labeled New Orleans Police Department visor. He looked like a toddler with freckles polluted on his face.

Gale stood up and walked behind the sketch artist. "Yikes, what's with the eyes?"

"That's what I see. They're hollowed out."

"I'll say. It gives me the creeps. Should I get Cory and Jesse to come in here?" Gale smiled wide.

"I think you'd better lay off the flirting with Commander Irons. You kept smiling at him during the introductions. Haven't you punished Tim enough?"

"No, I believe I have a few more hours of payback. Did you see the way he was staring and smiling at Miss Brigitte? He was acting like a fool. So, he's going to suffer a little while longer."

Gale left the office to find Cory and ignored Tim sitting at a corner desk.

Marie smiled at the sketch artist. "Sorry about that, she gets a bit wired when she has to compete against other women."

Cory entered the room first and sat next to Marie. "All finished?"

"Yep, it took me a while, but I feel comfortable with the similarities."

Jesse entered the room and stood behind the sketch artist. His tall, lean frame towered over everyone. His mussed ginger hair stopped at his shoulders. His hazel eyes were hidden behind the reflection of his GQ wire-rimmed glasses.

"This is what you saw in your visions?" Jesse slowly looked at Marie and then back at the sketch.

"Yes, I'd say that's an exact resemblance. Does this look like anyone involved in your case?" Marie placed her hand on Cory's thigh.

Jesse grabbed the sketch and looked up over the pad at Marie. "I thought the vision you saw would match up with one of the women found in one of our cold cases. But I'm a little confused. Did you say the visions you saw involved a satanic ritual and a voodoo dance?"

"Yes, that's what they were. Why? Doesn't this sketch match with anything you're involved in?"

"Yes, it does, but not with what I originally thought. This sketch here is our Jane Doe lying in our morgue at the medical center. They found her last Thursday." Jesse leaned against the wall.

"Had she been stabbed to death?" Marie shivered.

"Yes, but we hadn't identified any other signs of a satanic ritual."

Cory sat up in his chair. "Which are?"

"Well, there are all sorts of satanic ritual abuse. Beatings, electroshock, torture, forced infestation of drugs, blood, and feces." Jesse set the sketchpad down on the desk and dismissed the sketch artist.

"Oh, man, that's disgusting." Gale got up from her chair and looked out the door.

"None of these signs were found on your Jane Doe?" Cory grabbed Marie's hand.

"No, and there weren't any rope or chain marks on the wrists or feet either. Sometimes there is evidence of skinning."

Gale turned and looked at Jesse in shock. "Skinning? What is that?"

"It's one of the practices that take place in a satanic ritual. They scrape only the top layers of skin. There are so many types of satanic ritual abuse that it's sometimes hard to determine if that's what was involved or just some other type of abuse." Jesse sat down in his chair.

Marie nervously got up from her chair and stood next to Gale. "I know what I saw. I saw a woman in complete terror screaming and someone stabbing her in the heart with a dagger. It was a satanic ritual, and she was somehow involved in the voodoo dance."

"The tie in with the voodoo dance would tend to make sense. It's supposed to put someone in a spell or a trance to bewitch a person. But it's more of a religion."

"Religion? I always thought voodoo was evil." Cory shifted in his chair.

"No, actually voodoo means spirit or the religious communication with spirits. It's been used to help people with things like love spells and reduce anxiety or despair." Jesse leaned his elbow on the arm of his chair and looked at Marie. "If you saw this woman in both types of visions, it's possible she was practicing Satanism, and someone tried to help her through the voodoo healing dance."

Marie asked, "So the voodoo priestess I saw with a snake wrapped around her neck, and glowing eyes wasn't evil?"

"No, the snakes are considered holders of intuitive knowledge. They're also supposed to represent the balance between genders. As far as the glowing eyes, some say you never know the power and magic of voodoo." Jesse rubbed his jaw.

"If you don't mind me asking, what did you think my visions were originally about?"

"Well, right after Katrina, before my promotion, there were dead bodies of women left after the hurricane. But upon further investigation from the ME, the time of death was before Katrina hit. Plus, they had all the signs of satanic abuse." Jesse stared out the door. "It was massive chaos after that hurricane. There wasn't any time to do detail forensics on the bodies. The contusions around the wrists and the marks left behind from the electroshock made it obvious those women were murdered."

Cory asked, "How many women were there?"

"If my memory serves me right, around seven women. My commanding officer gave me the case because nobody wanted to delve into it. And there wasn't any time. So, my partner and I worked the case. We were able to identify all of the bodies, but we never found the murder or murderers." Jesse picked up the sketch pad. "With this sketch, I'm beginning to wonder now if we have a new case or just an old one starting up again."

Cory sat up in his chair and leaned on his knees. "Do you think you're going to have to reexamine your Jane Doe?"

"I think so. We're running it through IAFIS now."

Gale asked, "IAFIS, what is that? It sounds like the car company."

"IAFIS stands for Integrated Automated Fingerprint Identification System, which is an electronic exchange of fingerprint identification maintained by the FBI." Jesse looked at Marie. "If there's anything else you remember about these visions, don't hesitate to call me. Cory has my number."

"I won't, but I'm still getting a handle on all of this. I haven't experienced these types of visions. They're very powerful. We're planning on meeting the Big Easy Paranormal Society for dinner this evening with Delia Boisseau."

Jesse smiled. "Ah yes, Delia, she's a character. She's very well known in the French Quarter. André's a good man too. He's invited me along on some investigations, but I've never taken him up on it. I guess I still believe in scientific evidence."

"I know what you mean." Cory chuckled and looked at Marie. "I was the same way until I met this lady. I must tell you if Marie saw a woman being stabbed in her visions... it happened. Make no doubt about it."

Jesse shook his head. "Well, I'm starting to lean toward that idea because this hasn't been released to the public yet. So, if what my gut is telling me, and this is the same type of case as the one I had six years ago, then we'd better get ready for more bodies to start showing up."

Cory stood up and extended his hand to Jesse. "Thanks again for taking the time for us, and I hope we can help you out on this."

"I hope so too. It's great to see you. You've come a long way since the academy." Jesse shook Cory's hand.

Marie stood up and walked toward Gale. "Well, we'd better be on our way. We want to do some sightseeing. Maybe head down to Jackson Square Park."

Jesse walked them to the exit. "Stay in touch, and I'll be sure to do the same."

Gale winked at Jesse. "It was great to meet you."

Marie grabbed Gale's elbow. "Come on, flirting."

Cory pulled out his street map. "We may want to grab a taxi. It's a bit of a walk to the park."

"That sounds good because my feet are killing me." Gale rubbed her ankle.

"Maybe it would have been easier getting around in the rental car." Marie followed everyone toward the curb.

"No, I like walking around. You can see more." Tim tagged along behind Gale.

The taxi dropped them off in front of Jackson Square Park where street artists lined up along the iron fence. Each artist had their unique brand of art and displayed them on every square inch of space.

Marie admired the beautiful palm trees inside the park and sat down on a bench. She chuckled at the driver of a horse-drawn carriage wearing a Santa hat go by with tourists flashing their cameras and pointing at all of the sites. "We should take a ride in one of those carriages. I think it would be fun."

"No, thanks, I don't need to be sitting behind the ass of a horse." Gale continued to ignore Tim and chuckled.

"How long are you going to ignore me? I've apologized a million times. Can we please move on from this?" Tim stroked Gale's arm.

Gale looked at Tim and sighed. "Okay, but if I see you so much as look at that Brigitte woman, there's going to be trouble."

Tim leaned over and laid a lip-lock on Gale. "Consider my eyes frozen on you."

Marie looked at Gale. "Are you done now? You feel better?"

"Yep, and don't look at me as if I'm some crazy jealous woman. You'd be the same way if Cory were checking any other woman out. Am I right?"

Marie shrugged her shoulders and winked at Cory. "I've never been given a reason to get jealous."

Cory smiled and kissed Marie on the cheek. "I'm glad that's all settled. Can we get back to the Jane Doe lying in the morgue? How much do you believe is tied in with your visions? Do you think you'll be able to pick up on any more information?"

"I have no idea. Maybe when we sit down with Delia this evening, she'll be able to help us out." Marie stood up and began to sway to the sexy jazz music coming from a street vendor playing the saxophone.

Gale leaned forward on her knees. "Do you think she'll give me a reading?"

Marie turned around. "Why haven't you ever asked me to give you a reading?"

Gale looked at Marie with raised eyebrows. "I don't know. I never really thought about it. Can you give me one?"

"I suppose I never really thought about it either. How strange is that?" Marie chuckled and continued to sway to the music. "I have to say that I feel more relaxed than I did. I've been meditating more, and I've got my crystal with me. I haven't said much to any of you, but there are a whole lot of ghosts roaming around New Orleans."

Gale shot up from the bench. "Shut the front door. Are you kidding me? You can see ghosts walking around now?"

"Yeah, I think a few have realized I can see them, and they look intrigued by me. Some are mean looking and ignore me." Marie pointed across the street to a group of people sitting down at a table, having lunch. "See those people sitting over there at the café? There's a woman repeatedly dancing around them and laughing. She's wearing a pale blue dress that reminds me of the roaring twenties. She has a sequenced blue band around her head with a small feather poking out from it, and there are pearls coiled around her neck. Her lipstick is bright red. She looks like a flapper."

Gale gawked across the street and then back at Marie. "I can't believe this. I'm so jealous. What a cool ability you have."

Marie's smile faded. "Yes, at this particular moment, it is fun, but the last two visions I've experienced were not. Trust me, this isn't cool."

Gale walked over and draped her arm around Marie's shoulders. "Yeah, you're right, I'm sorry. I forgot about those. But do you think you can fill me in on when you do see something cool?"

Marie laughed. "Yes, I suppose so."

Cory got up from the bench. "I'm ready for some lunch. Do you all want to head back to the Napoleon House? Those sandwiches looked pretty good last night."

"Oooh yeah, that sounds great." Gale turned to Tim and grabbed his arm. "How about you? Are you ready for some lunch, as if I need to ask?"

Tim smiled. "Of course, and I could go for a beer right now too."

Marie's cell phone rang, and she pulled it from her purse. "Hello? André, how are you? Yes, I did meet with the sketch artist. It was fascinating. Tonight at six would be great. Yes, I know where it is. Thank you again for allowing us to meet with Ms. Boisseau. I can fill you all in on what happened this morning at the police department. Great, see you then. Goodbye."

Gale asked, "Where are we meeting everyone?"

"At O'Brien's, it's a pub on Bourbon Street. I remember passing it last week. It looks like a fun place. André said we could get a table on the patio. He claims that'll be a little more private. He was curious about what happened with the sketch artist."

"Well let's get some lunch now and maybe do a little more

sightseeing. I wouldn't mind taking a tour of the Cajun Country." Cory held Marie's hand.

"Hey yeah, that sounds like fun. I think there's a company that gives you a boat tour of the cypress swamps." Marie followed everyone toward the Cathedral.

"It doesn't matter to me, just as long as I get something to eat now." Tim caught Gale's placated look and smiled.

They walked toward Chartres Street and stopped in front of a gospel singer performing on the corner. Her song was solemn and pure and made your heart ache at the complexity of her words. Time seemed to stop, and nothing else existed but her voice.

"Wow, now she can sing. What an amazing voice." Gale swayed slowly to the melody.

"I'll say. I don't think I've ever heard anything like it." Tim smiled at Gale and placed his hands on her hips.

Marie felt herself get lost in the music, and her mind began to drift in and out of consciousness. She saw a young dark-haired girl walk across the street toward her crying and wiping her eyes. The girl approached Marie and asked, help me, oh please make them stop. Marie asked, "What happened to you? Who are you talking about?"

Gale looked at Marie. "What? Are you talking to me?"

Marie remained in a trance and watched the girl fade in and out and then finally disappear. "Wow, that was weird."

"What just happened?" Cory was holding Marie's shoulders and looked into her eyes.

"I just saw a ghost of a dark-haired girl crying and asking me to help her and to make them stop. But I felt a pain in my abdomen and that same drugged feeling I had in my first vision. It was like I was seeing and hearing her, but also feeling some other presence all around her." Marie walked over to a bench in front of St. Louis Cathedral and sat down.

Cory sat down, and his cell phone rang. "Hello? Hey, Jesse, how are you? No, we were just headed over for some lunch at the Napoleon House. I see. Yeah, I can ask her. Did you? Really? Okay, we'll meet you there in a couple of hours. Yeah, see ya, then."

"What did Jesse want?" Marie closed her eyes and rubbed her temples.

"He wanted to know if you had any visions lately. They found another body of a young woman in an alley off of Canal Street."

Marie quickly looked up at Cory. "Are you kidding me? What did he say she looked like?"

"He didn't, but he wants us to meet him in his office after lunch. The time of death was around three in the morning." Cory cupped Marie's face in his hands. "Marie, what he did say was the woman they found had been sliced in the abdomen and placenta was left behind along with an umbilical cord. The woman was pregnant."

Gale turned and almost tripped over the bench leg. "Are you serious? Marie, you just said you had a pain in your abdomen. Do you think what you just saw was the same woman?"

"I don't know, but as always it's too much of a coincidence. We don't believe in those, remember? But what would taking a baby have anything to do with a satanic ritual?"

"Well, I have read where they will take the baby as a sacrifice. They supposedly impregnate one of their victims from one of the occult members and then sacrifice the baby." Tim sat next to Marie and handed her a bottle of water.

"Okay, again, I need to start screening your television programs." Gale knelt in front of Marie. "Are you okay? You look a little gray."

"Well, I do think I need to eat some lunch. Why don't we

get something to eat and then head over to the police station? I suspect he'll want me to identify the body?" Marie stood up and waited for her head to stop spinning.

"He didn't say so, but I would imagine he would." Cory put his arm around Marie's waist. "Hang onto me until you get your bearings. The Napoleon House is only a few blocks away."

As they headed down the street, Marie couldn't get the dark-haired woman out of her mind. There were so many questions running through her head, and she knew that before she went to the police, she needed to call Myra. This was all beginning to overwhelm her, and she needed to be grounded. Myra was her only hope in that department.

SIX

"I still don't believe we should have left her on Canal Street. I told you we should have dumped her over the Mississippi line. I think it was careless. Plus, I don't think we needed to use the baby as a sacrifice." She nervously rubbed her neck.

"We didn't have any time. We barely made the three a.m. timeframe. It doesn't matter, what's done is done. The baby was needed as a sacrifice to Beelzebub. You need to stop obsessing over trivial issues such as this and keep your mind focused on our goal." He rubbed his jaw and stared at her through narrowed eyes. "It sounds as though you're having second thoughts on our objective. Do I hear a little fear in your voice?"

She stood up and walked over to the window. "No, I'm not having second thoughts. I understand what was needed. I hope nobody finds the baby's remains."

"That's impossible. It was crucified and burned. We left no trails."

She chuckled softly and turned around. "There's always a trail. You'd better remember that. Jesse Irons is on this case.

And now he's involved that psychic from Sullivan's Island. I told you about her."

"Yes, I've been hearing the rumors about her. You're not the only one who has this information. We have plenty of people from the angelic court that keep me informed." He rose and walked behind her and began stroking her thigh. "Come, let's go and rejoice in our sacrifice. No more talk of these others. We have much still to do to please the hierarchy."

She smiled and turned toward him and kissed him hard on the lips. She felt his hands squeeze her arms, and his nails dug into her skin. When he pulled away, she saw where he had drawn blood. She wiped the blood with her finger and placed it on his lips. He slowly licked her finger, and they both laughed and walked out together to finish what they had begun.

MARIE HELD onto Cory's hand and squeezed tight while she slowly watched the ME pull the sheet down below the woman's chin. "That's her. That's the woman I just saw on the street in my vision. Oh, Cory, that's horrible." She turned away and buried her face in his shoulders.

Cory nodded at the ME and walked. Marie passed Jesse over to a chair in the hall. "Are you going to be okay?"

"I don't know. I'm not sure what I'm feeling right now." Marie looked into Cory's eyes. "How do you deal with this sort of thing on your job?"

"It's difficult. You eventually become numb, but it never really leaves you." Cory looked at Jesse. "What do we do now?"

"We wait until we get more information from the medical examiner's report. We've identified our first Jane Doe. Her name is Anna Beth Montgomery from Valdosta, Georgia. We're waiting for her family to confirm her identity." Jesse pulled a chair in front of Marie and sat down. "Marie, I don't normally put much stock in these visions or anything paranormal. But I consider you to be pretty grounded. Not to mention, I trust Cory's judgment. But in this latest vision, did the victim say anything to you?"

Marie looked up and saw her reflection in his glasses. "Yes, she was crying. She was asking me to help her and to make them stop."

"And nothing else, anything that may have stood out for you?"

"No, except I did feel this pain in my abdomen. And I felt as if I was drugged. Myra told me spirits would sometimes transfer what they're feeling." Marie saw Jesse's confused expression. "Oh, Myra's a very dear friend of mine. She's a member of SIPS and a psychic medium as well."

"I see, well once we run her prints through IAFIS and get the final report. I'll want to talk with you some more." Jesse looked at Cory. "Any chance you can give me some man hours on this? I may need all of the help I can get."

"Consider it done. I'm already tied into this case." Cory smiled at Marie.

Jesse stood up and shifted the chair against the wall with his foot. "Great, thanks. I'll stay in touch, and in the meantime, if anything else develops on your end, I'm available twenty-four seven."

Cory shook Jesse's hand. "Ditto, we'll talk to you soon. I think we're going to head back to the hotel a bit before we meet up with BEPS and Delia Boisseau for dinner this evening. I think Marie needs some rest."

Marie leaned her head on Cory's shoulder and walked with him through the big steel doors. "I need to call Myra again when we get back to the hotel. After that, I'm taking a nap. I'm completely exhausted."

Gale stood up and greeted Marie at the top of the stairs.

"How was it? Was it the same woman you saw in your vision? Was it gross?"

Marie picked her head up and gave a faint smile. "It was horrible and yes to the rest of your questions."

"Oh, wow, did they say anything about it being a sacrifice?" Tim patted Marie on the shoulder.

Cory replied, "No, they'll fill us in on the final report. They also need to run her prints through the database and find out who she is. Jesse asked me to help them with the case."

"I can't believe this. We're in the middle of another serial killer or killers." Gale looked at Marie and stopped walking. "I'm sorry, I didn't mean to sound so negative. I know this isn't your fault. How are you holding up?"

"I'm exhausted, and I need to call Myra as soon as we get back to the hotel. Then I'm going to take a nap before our dinner this evening."

"I agree. Do you want to Skype or call her?" Gale walked in step with Marie.

"If you don't mind, I'd rather talk to her alone. I need to focus on all of this, and I still get too distracted when others are around." Marie noticed Gale's hurt expression. "You understand, don't you? It's nothing personal. Myra has a way of calming me and talking me through the things I'm still learning."

"Of course, of course, I understand. I'm just worried about you. I wish there were more I could do. I feel so helpless."

Marie smiled. "Thank you for understanding, and please realize you have helped me more than you will ever know just by being my friend and supporting me. You know that."

Gale grinned and stuffed her hands into her jean pockets. "Aw shucks, what can I say? That's what I do."

. . .

Marie felt happy and refreshed as she walked in with Cory to the patio bar at O'Brien's. Her high heeled pumps sounded like tap shoes against the slate flooring. The open air and lush foliage gave the appearance of someone's backyard instead of a restaurant. The fountain sitting in the center of the patio bar had flames shooting out from the center that danced against the splashing water.

Myra placed Marie into a relaxed state and helped her to nap devoid of any visions or dreams. It was the best she had felt in months. She even felt a bit sexy in her gray tweed pencil skirt and sleeveless ruffled top. It exposed her swim toned arms. She smiled at Cory, playing with the tips of her blonde hair as it rolled down over her shoulders.

Cory leaned over to Marie and whispered in her ear. "You look very relaxed... and very sexy. I'm glad Myra was able to help you. Are you going to share any of that conversation with Delia?"

"I'm not sure yet. I want to learn a little more about Delia, although Myra didn't have any reservations about her."

Gale stared a hole through Brigitte and tapped Marie on the shoulder. "Do you see the way she's been looking at André? I think the two of them have something going on."

"I would think that would make you happy, considering you thought she was after Tim." Marie winked and took another sip of her wine.

"Yeah, well, I'm over that now. She seems shifty to me. I get an odd vibe from her." Gale grabbed a catfish strip off of the appetizer plate. "Can you pick up anything on her?"

"Pick up anything on her? You mean like, does she wear a chastity belt or boots to bed?" Marie shifted out of the way of Gale's elbow.

"No, I mean use your ability to find something out about her. You know, is she wanted for robbing a bank or something?"

Marie looked at Gale and rolled her eyes. "Are you serious? Robbing a bank? No, I'm not getting anything from her. My ability doesn't work that way. At least I don't think so. I'm still getting a grasp on all of this, so let's change the subject and try to get in on their conversations."

Gale frowned. "Well, I have to say they're an interesting group, aren't they? I mean what's your take on Philippe? He sounded French to me."

"Yes, I think he is. It'll be interesting to investigate with him. I love how there are so many different personalities interested in ghost hunting."

Gale took a sip of Chablis. "Yeah, well I'm thrown off by Jason. Who would have thought he'd be interested in anything paranormal? He hacked on André quite a bit, don't ya think?"

"Yeah, he's a little abrupt. I think Katherine seems nice enough. She seems to have a lot of knowledge of ghost hunting. I got the impression she's their tech person." Marie popped a fry in her mouth and made a mental note to hit the pool in the morning.

Delia heartily laughed at everyone and smiled at André. "Boy, ya be tellin' stories on me now. What would ya maw be thinkin' of ya? Ya best keep them to ya' self."

André chuckled and tapped a fork on his wine glass. "Can I have your attention, please? Now that we've all had a chance to have our drinks and appetizers, I thought we'd start some preliminary questions that any of you may have for Delia before our entrées arrive. She has told me she is willing to do readings on anyone and answer any questions you may have. I always like to get Delia to do a protection prayer on our team before we go on a ghost investigation which she will perform before we leave here this evening." He took a sip of wine and looked at Tim. "Would anyone from SIPS like to begin?"

Tim's eyes widened like a deer in headlights. "Oh, well, I

guess I can go first. I'm not sure if I have any questions, though."

Delia held up her hand and closed her eyes. "Ya have much light around ya, and ya have a deep soul. I can see how very faithful ya are to da woman in ya life. Ya were a warrior in ya previous life. Ya gave much protection to dose around ya. Ya may need to protect yourself again."

Tim asked, frantically. "Again... when and how?"

"I don't know, I feel somethin' blockin' me now, but I will give ya extra protection. In da meantime, if ya ever feel or see someone starin' at ya in da eyes, picture a brick wall and close ya mind." Delia opened her eyes and smiled.

Tim gulped and replied, "Thank you, I'll be sure to do that."

Gale blurted, "Do me next. I want to know what you see for me."

Delia's eyes narrowed. "Ya needs to give dis poor boy a break and know dat he loves ya."

Everyone laughed, and the readings were interrupted by the servers bringing their meals. They ate their dinners and continued their conversations about voodoo, ghost investigations, and psychic mediums. Marie tried to ignore Delia's stare and practiced the brick wall in her own mind. She could feel herself getting light headed and decided she wasn't going to allow anyone to read or control her mind.

Delia took a sip of lemon water and looked at Marie. "Ya done a great job at blockin' me chile. Ya have a powerful will and mind. Dat's what ya need to do when ya feel a vision takin' ya over. Don't let yaself fall into da vision. Picture dat brick wall or a circle of inverted mirrors around ya. It'll cast away any unwanted evil."

Marie smiled. "Thank you. I've also been practicing my

meditation. I need to get stronger in that area. I'm learning to clear my thoughts."

"Dat's right. I can tell." Delia touched the middle of her forehead between her brows. "Ya have to keep da third eye clear. It can show ya da way."

Marie set her fork down. "Why do you think I'm being sought out from these women in my visions?"

The group stopped talking as Delia lean forward. "Cause ya have a purpose chile. Ya heart is big, and da other side knows it. But ya still not acceptin' all of it. I can see ya strugglin' ta understand. But ya will. When da time is right, ya will."

The evening ended with a protection prayer from Delia and wishes of a good night's rest until they met again at the LaLaurie House. Marie and the SIPS team talked back to the hotel about the readings Delia gave on everyone. Especially the insight she gave to Marie. Marie felt a little more relaxed, but still had a feeling of the unknown. It was odd realizing she may very well hold the key, yet again, to find the people who murdered these two women in such a horrific manner.

SEVEN

THE WOMAN in Myra's dream could smell incense burn her nostrils, making her lethargic and nauseous. As she slowly focused her eyes on the circle of candles burning around her, she could taste the vinegar from the gag that was tightly bound in her mouth. Her arms and legs were spread apart and strapped down at her wrists and ankles, which scraped against the damp rough surface when she tried to wriggle free. There was an odor of earth and decay emanating through the room, and when she saw the pentagram appear through the shadows on the stone wall, she began to scream.

From out of nowhere, there were hooded, robed figures chanting and moving around her in a repeated circle. She found herself getting dizzy as the characters began to blur and sway, causing her to fall into a trance. Just as she felt herself start to black out, someone struck her legs, stomach, and arms with a knife. She wasn't able to determine if this was real or a dream. But as soon as the nude man wearing a ram's head appeared at her feet holding a knife, she suddenly realized she was in the middle of a nightmare.

. . .

GALE STARED at the LaLaurie House and shrugged her shoulders. "I'm sorry, I don't see it. How in the world is this place haunted? It's the most beautiful house I've ever seen." She turned toward André. "How did you get permission to investigate this house from the owner?"

André smiled. "I know the real estate agent well. It's taken me two years to get the owner's approval, so this is a real milestone for us. And yes, I agree, it is a beautiful home and completely misleading as a haunted house."

Marie strained her neck to see the three-story gray stucco façade with its second story encased in a black wrought iron balcony. The white painted trim and black shutters were a beautiful complimentary contrast. "Each floor has its own unique style. As if it were three separate houses combined in one."

"Yes, well, wait until you see the inside. It's magnificent. We're going to have a lot of equipment to set up in some very interesting areas." Katherine waved at a striking redheaded woman approaching them wearing a navy-blue pantsuit with navy spiked heeled pumps. "Cassandra, thank you for meeting us. We appreciate the time and effort you have put into arranging our investigation."

"Oh, think nothing of it. It was my pleasure. Besides, I'm just dying to see what you catch on video, or on one of those voice recorder thingy's." Cassandra Williams was a prominent real estate agent for the LaLaurie House and very well known in New Orleans.

Marie whispered in Gale's ear. "Gee Gale... she sounds just like you when you describe our equipment."

"Very funny. I know what it's called. It's an electronic voice phenomenon recorder, EVP recorder for short." Gale stuck out her tongue and wrinkled her nose.

Cassandra walked them to the side of the building and

slipped the key into the lockbox attached to the iron-gated door. "Now André I have your promise to be careful where you place your equipment and to leave no traces of anything, correct?"

"Yes, Cassandra, you won't even know we were here." André winked and held the gate open for everyone.

Marie stepped into the foyer and gawked at the spiral staircase and the black and white checked marble floor. "Wow, now this is an entry that would capture any buyer. Check out these faux painted walls. They're scored and painted to look like ivory marble."

Cory stumbled behind Marie, pulling a sizeable hard suitcase on rollers. "Did you happen to see all of the equipment they have in their van? Philippe was gathering things that I've never seen before. They have some new digital recorder that records with the quality of a CD. A bunch of night vision video lights that attach to the video cameras, and a laser grid. You had talked about getting one of those."

"This will be a perfect outlet for us to test how the equipment works. I've already put a few of those things on my wish list." Marie smiled and helped carry another bag Tim handed her.

Brigitte struggled with the bag strapped over her shoulder and plopped it on the foyer floor. "How is it we women get stuck carrying the biggest bags? Wow, get a load of this place. Didn't Cassandra say there was some activity in the foyer? How in the world are we going to get the right angle on that staircase?"

Jason rolled another suitcase past Brigitte and wiped the sweat from his brow with his forearm. "I was invited here to a party a while back. You can get lost in some of these rooms. Does anyone know where command central is going to be?"

"I think it's going to be on the patio... wherever that is.

André said you need to walk through the room with the green leather chairs and then out the back." Brigitte ran her hand along the walls and continued through the doorway.

The team worked diligently organizing all of their equipment in just the right locations. They were all handed separate notes that the BEPS team took on their initial walk-through. Marie was impressed by how thorough they were. Everyone worked together like a well-oiled machine, and they were cautious not to damage any of the areas where they placed the equipment. Once everyone learned where the claims of paranormal activity took place, they decided it was time to go dark and break into teams of twos and threes, leaving someone at command central to watch the main camera views.

Marie held a K-II meter and walked with Cory and Katherine into the dining area. "I could probably entertain my entire family in this room. Check out the chandelier. Katherine, what were the claims again in here?"

"There were accounts of full-bodied apparitions and hearing voices. Some claim they've seen Madame Delphine herself." Katherine placed her mini-DVD on the table. "Why don't we sit quietly for a few moments to get a feel first, and then we can try and see if there is anyone here with us."

Cory sat next to Marie and whispered in her ear. "I'm not sure I know the difference between a full-bodied apparition and one that isn't."

Marie smiled in the dark. "A full-bodied apparition is just that. It is a full-sized translucent human being giving off a soft white glow. These ghosts are also seen in reflective surfaces like mirrors or windows. Partial apparitions will normally only reveal their upper torso and arms. This type of ghost is a lot more prevalent than a full body apparition due to the additional energy needed to appear in full form."

Katherine replied, "That's correct. Then you have your

shadow people who are often considered a dark force entity or demon. These ghosts can take the general shape of a being, but sometimes seen as a blob of black smoke. Some entities appear as mist or fog but move more intelligently. Orbs are the most often documented occurrence in ghost hunting, and probably the most debated. The orb was debunked as nothing more than an energy particle or dust. There is no conclusive evidence that an orb is a spirit of any kind. And then you have swimmers who are very similar to energy rods, but they have what appear to be fins all around the rod. No one knows what these things are. I could give you a lot more information on energy rods, but I won't bore you anymore."

Marie asked, "Wow, Katherine, you have quite a scientific approach to the paranormal, where did you learn all of this?"

"I took a course and got my certification as a paranormal investigator. I've always had a fascination with the paranormal ever since I had my first encounter when I was fourteen. The home my family lived in the bayou was haunted."

"I'm beginning to feel left out on not having had any personal experiences." Cory shifted in his chair.

Marie heard a knock on the wall. "What was that? Did you hear that?"

"Yes, I did," Katherine spoke into the dark. "Is there anyone here with us this evening? It sounds as though you are trying to get our attention. I suppose we were talking too much for you."

"I just saw a shadow. Wow, I never saw a shadow before. It went from left to right past that entryway." Cory grabbed onto Marie's hand.

"I saw it too. Was that you Madame Delphine? Are you trying to get our attention? I think you need to do more than that. Why don't you come over and touch one of us? Or do something more to let us know you are here." Marie watched the lights flicker on the K-II meter and got up from her chair and moved over to the fireplace.

Katherine set a recorder on the table and tapped on it. "You can come over and talk into this device. It will record anything you would like to tell us."

"We want to talk with you. Are you angry we are here in your home?" Marie moved over and stood behind Cory. "I'm getting a read in here. I haven't had this type of experience on an investigation, but I can see Madame Delphine as plain as day standing over in the corner between those two windows. She isn't looking too happy."

"Are you seeing her?" Cory got up from his chair and stood beside Marie. "What's she doing?"

"She's just staring me down with a frown on her face."

Suddenly a picture flew off the wall and landed on the floor and broke into pieces.

Marie jumped. "She's gone. She just threw that picture off the wall. She's a temperamental ghost, isn't she?"

Katherine spoke into the recorder. "Be sure to document when the picture hit the floor to any possible voice phenomenon's that may have occurred at the same time."

"I can't believe you saw her. You've never done that before, have you?" Cory was rubbing Marie's shoulder.

"No, I have to say that was a new one for me. I'm beginning to get a better handle on opening my third eye as Myra and Delia instructed me to do." Marie shivered. "Wow, I'm not sure where Madame Delphine went, but she was in a hurry and looked pretty pissed off that we're here."

Katherine spoke into the recorder. "End EVP session in the dining room. Why don't we send in another team? I want to check with Brigitte at command central to see if she saw anything on camera of the picture falling."

"Speaking of which, Cassandra isn't going to be too happy when she finds out about that picture, is she?" Cory followed Marie out of the room.

"No, we may have to pay to have the glass replaced. But that's okay, especially if we can show them some evidence." Katherine turned off the DVD camera and followed them to the patio.

Gale walked over to Marie beside one of the tall potted plants. "You are never going to guess what Tim, Philippe, and I just heard in the room with those funky red velvet chairs. Which by the way, side note, Philippe is so cool, he told us about one of his exploits to Africa. He floated up some river that begins with a Z and saw some awesome waterfalls and crocodiles. I love his French accent. It's so much nicer than Brigitte's fake southern one."

Tim corrected, "The Zambezi River."

"What? Oh, yeah, right, whatever. It sounded awesome." Gale poked Tim in the arm.

Marie tapped Gale on the shoulder. "What did you hear?"

"I didn't hear anything. I'd love to take a trip to Africa."

Marie sighed. "No, I mean, what did you hear in the room with the funky red velvet chairs?"

"Oh that, sorry we heard this deep sigh or a groan, and then the words get out. Can you believe it? We played it back, and it was creepy." Gale leaned over and took off her spiked heels. "Man, my feet are killing me in these things."

Brigitte leaned toward Gale. "I told you those weren't investigation shoes. You need to wear comfortable shoes. Y'all never know where you're going to step in those things."

Gale glared back at Brigitte. "Yes, I know what you told me, but I believe in looking good wherever I go. Isn't that right, Tim?"

Tim answered on command. "Yes, of course, and you always look fantastic."

Gale smiled wide at Brigitte and tilted her head. "See, so

don't worry about me. I'm just fine."

Marie interrupted the visible hen fight beginning by stepping between the two women. "Brigitte, can you play back for us camera number three when we were in the dining room? We were hoping you caught the picture that fell off of the wall."

"A picture fell off the wall? Whoa, that's pretty cool. You tend to have that happen to you a lot on investigations. The same thing happened to you in the Poe Library at home with books flying off of the shelves." Gale nudged Marie with her elbow.

"Yeah, well, I also saw Madame LaLaurie in the corner. She's the one who knocked the picture off. She seems to be a bit perturbed about us being here."

"You saw Delphine? Wow, is she as scary looking as her picture?" Tim leaned against the temporary command post folding table.

"Scarier, and I'm hoping we may have captured something as evidence." Marie turned back to the screen and watched Brigitte play back to when Marie was by the fireplace. "That's it. There it is, did you all see that?"

André's eyes got wide. "I sure did. What the heck happened in there? Man, how am I going to explain that to Cassandra?"

Cory chuckled. "That's what we said. Katherine said they might not mind it so much after seeing the evidence and learning it was Delphine herself who knocked it off the wall."

André asked, "How do you know that?"

Marie replied, "Because I saw her do it, and she isn't a happy camper. After she knocked it off the wall, she disappeared right out of the room. We wanted another team to go in the dining room to see what they come up with."

André stared at Marie for a few seconds and nodded. "Right, okay. How about I stay here at command central and

Brigitte, you and Jason go to the dining room. Katherine, how about you and your team go check out the kitchen. Philippe, can you all head over to the card room with the small round table and all of those odd marble statues?"

Gale whispered in Marie's ear. "Have you seen any other ghosts? Isn't this something new for you on an investigation?"

Marie nodded. "Yeah, that's what Cory and I were saying. But no, I haven't seen any other ghosts. But the night is still young."

They all broke out into their destinations and continued to document, debunk, and record as much information as possible. Each group shared their individual experiences and made sure to jot down notes needed to compare to any footage caught on video or recorders.

At the end of the investigation, the group split up again to recover all of the equipment in the same organized fashion as they did placing it. They carefully removed the masking tape from the floors and walls and returned any furniture that may have been moved for ease during the investigation.

Marie walked toward the patio carrying the laser grid and remembered Gale saying how well it caught a shadow moving through it. Just as she approached the patio door, she felt the same tingling sensation shoot up both of her arms, and the room became dark and cold. Marie could see her breath and again smelled the fragrance of sandalwood mixed with decay and death. The scene changed, and she was standing in the middle of a room with dimly lit candles that had melted down to an inch in size. There was a decrepit above-ground crypt in the middle of the candles and Marie spotted blood still wet dripping over the edge and down the sides of the tomb. To her left on the wall was a faintly painted pentagram which looked to have been there for ages.

Marie cautiously approached the grave site when out of the

corner of her right eye, a woman screamed at her holding out her hands and crying for help. The tears that ran down her pasty pale face were red, and her eyes were hollow and black. Her long blonde hair was matted and tangled in a horrifying mass on her head. The young woman fell to her knees and pleaded with Marie to help her. When Marie tried to touch her, the woman began to melt, and within seconds she sizzled into a puddle of ash.

EIGHT

MARIE DROPPED TO HER KNEES, and the decaying room disappeared when she heard Cory and Gale's voice yelling for her to open her eyes. As she did, she saw everyone staring back at her while her head rested in Cory's lap. "What happened? And why am I on the floor?"

"We might ask you the same thing." Cory helped Marie sit up. "You had another vision, didn't you? Who was it this time?"

Marie leaned against Cory and looked at Gale. "I don't know who it was, but it was another woman pleading for my help. Oh, it was awful. She was in some creepy looking crypt or mausoleum, and right before I could go to her, she melted."

"She what? Just like the wicked witch in the Wizard of Oz?" Gale reached over and straightened out Marie's shirt collar.

"Yeah, you could compare it like that. But there's no doubt it had the same occult theme going on. Candles were burning all around this tomb, and there was a pentagram on the wall." Marie tried to stand and couldn't seem to find her legs. "And I smelled that same incense burning, but it smelled of flesh burning or death. Oh, and there was blood all over the tomb too."

André helped Cory lift Marie to a chair. "Well, I'd say we can call it a night. I think you need to go back to your hotel and get some rest. You've had quite an evening, what with seeing Madame LaLaurie and now this."

Gale looked at André. "You sound as if you don't believe Marie. And I take offense to that."

"No, no, Gale, it's okay. He's right. It's been quite an evening." Marie looked at Cory. "Let's head back to the hotel. I want to call Jesse in the morning to see if anyone showed up at the morgue."

"You think what you just saw has some correlation with someone being murdered in a satanic ritual?" Brigitte sat down next to Katherine.

"Look if my friend said she saw something... then she saw something. We don't take kindly to strangers questioning her ability." Gale stood up and looked down at Brigitte.

Tim put his arm around Gale and pulled her back. "Okay, well, that's enough for one night. Why don't we all head back to the hotel, and we can work out a time to go over the evidence?"

"That sounds like a good idea." Philippe stood up and pressed his hands against his wrinkled jeans. "It was great working with all of you this evening. I think it was fascinating."

Katherine stood up. "I agree. I look forward to seeing what we caught."

Marie got her bearings and held Cory's hand tight. "Can you give us a day or two? We want to help, but I'd also like to check into this vision a little more."

"That's fine. We all have day jobs to attend to as well. How does Thursday mid-afternoon sound?" André looked at Jason.

"Will that work for you? Are there any events that need the upstairs room?"

Jason shook his head. "No, no parties going on this week. Let's meet for lunch. I can have Candy make up some food for us." Jason walked over to Marie. "Are you sure you're okay? I can see your color is coming back a little. But you looked pretty pale a few minutes ago."

Marie smiled. "I'm fine and thank you for asking. These latest visions really drain me."

"I can't even imagine. I never believed in any of this stuff myself until my wife—" Jason stopped in mid-sentence. "Let's just say I'm a believer now."

"We've all had some sort of personal experience. That's why we do what we do." Tim smiled and put his arm around Gale. "Come on, let's go, it's late, and I think we're going to need some sleep."

"Yeah, I'm ready." Gale turned to the group but ignored Brigitte and André. "Good night, everyone, or is it morning? Anyway, we'll see you all on Thursday."

Marie waved and felt her cell phone vibrate in her pocket. "Who would be calling me at this hour? Oh, wait, it's Myra. Hello Myra, what on earth are you doing up at this hour? Yes, I'm fine. Did you see her too? What time was this? Interesting, mine just happened about five minutes ago. No, I'm fine, really I am, but I'm exhausted. We just got done with our investigation here at the LaLaurie House, and we're heading back to the hotel. Yes, I'll tell everyone. I'm going to call Jesse tomorrow and see if anyone showed up in the morgue. I will, I promise. We'll call you later, say around ten? Thanks, Myra. Good night."

"What did she want?" Cory brushed Marie's bangs off of her forehead.

"She saw the same vision as me. She said she dreamt the

same vision of that poor young woman in that horrible crypt. Only it felt as if it was herself going through it. She also got some other readings or thoughts from the woman. She couldn't quite explain it, but she almost felt as if this woman is well known. Now I'm anxious to get a hold of Jesse." Marie walked out the door with everyone and wrapped her arms around Cory's waist. "Come on, let's all head back to the hotel before the sun comes up."

THE LIGHT PEERED through the window as Marie's eyes slowly came to focus on the elaborate paisley wallpaper and matching curtains. She could feel Cory's arm draped over her waist, creating a sense of comfort and contentment. She barely had any time to enjoy this mini-vacation with all of the added turmoil. What amazed her was how Cory completely accepted her and her ability. She wasn't even sure herself how to deal with all of her new psychic capabilities. It was calming to have Myra in her life to guide her, but it was especially perfect having a man in her life to roll with the punches.

Cory squeezed her hip. "Good morning, sunshine. Is there ever a morning you don't wake up before me?"

Marie rolled over and smiled at his brown eyes, staring back at her. She loved his muscle toned shoulders and narrow waist. "I guess not. But I've only been lying here for a few minutes. I was just thinking how wonderful you are to be putting up with all of this, and me. It's cut into our vacation."

Cory pulled Marie closer and kissed her cheek. "I'm certainly not putting up with you, and I'm having a blast on this vacation. You need to quit thinking about me and relax. We had some amazing experiences on the investigation. Don't you think?"

"Oh yes, and that laser grid was incredible. We have got to

get one of those. Gale said they were picking up some interesting conversations with one of the slaves on that spirit box Philippe was using. I can't wait to see the evidence." Marie rolled to the edge of the bed and sat up. "Should we call Jesse before we head over to the police department, or can we just go over?"

Cory chuckled and walked over to stand in front of Marie. "I know you're anxious to get over there, and we will. But first, I think we need to have a good breakfast, and I thought you might want to chat with Myra a little more."

"Oh yeah, I do. I'm going to video chat with her and the team to fill them in on the investigation and my vision." Marie watched Cory slip on his jeans and enjoyed the view. "Maybe we are getting up too early and should go back to bed for a while."

Cory grinned and jumped back into bed. "I concur. We need all the rest we can get."

Marie giggled at Cory's tickling and tried to wriggle out of his reach. "You know how ticklish I am." Her cheek caught the side of his face as his lips trailed down the side of her neck. "Yeah, I think Myra and the team can wait."

Cory stopped kissing Marie at the sound of the door knock. "Ignore that. If we don't answer, they'll go away."

"You seriously think Gale is going to leave?" Marie kissed Cory's nose and got up to slip into her robe and yelled at the back of the door. "We can hear you, stop banging on the door."

Gale pushed through the opened door past Marie and rolled her eyes. "You don't have time for any hanky panky this morning. Besides, you should have taken care of that last night as we did."

Tim looked at Marie and shrugged his shoulders while plopping down into the sofa. "What can I say, the woman has needs."

Marie shook her head. "Oh, she has needs alright. We didn't even have breakfast yet. Plus, I wanted to catch a swim before we left."

"You can do all of that. I've already ordered room service to be sent here. And yes, I put it on my room tab." Gale grabbed Marie's laptop and set it on the coffee table. "What's your password?"

"Oh, by all means, help yourself." Marie turned the screen to face her and typed the password. "And don't be giving me that look. You wouldn't give up your password either. Myra should have gathered everyone together by now. I miss having everyone around when we do an investigation. It's not the same, is it?"

"No, but I don't mind not having Harry around. He's a pain." Gale sat down on the sofa next to Tim ignoring Marie's exasperated look. "These rooms are great, aren't they? They're huge."

"Gale, don't change the subject, you need to lighten up on Harry. He's a great addition to the team, and you know that. I don't think you're happy unless you're arguing with someone. Only this time, it's Brigitte."

"Hey, wait a minute. I was giving her the benefit of the doubt until she started making comments about my shoes. Plus, don't you think she and André were a bit cynical about your vision? That ticked me off." Gale folded her arms and rested them on her chest.

"Yeah, I picked up on that too. I would have thought with André's relationship with Ms. Boisseau, he would be more accepting of what happened to you last evening." Cory rubbed the back of his neck and sat on the arm of the sofa. "Although I thought it was pretty cool how Jason seemed concerned. I wonder what happened to his wife."

"Yeah, he is pretty nice. Gale and I got the chance to investigate with him. He's really laid back." Tim shifted on the cushion and rubbed Gale's arm.

The laptop rang, and Myra's face appeared wearing a silk fuchsia scarf on her head. "Good morning, everyone. How are you all doing today? Did you get enough sleep from your investigation?"

Marie smiled. "Hello, Myra and yes, I think we did. How are all of you today?"

Jim piped up and shifted their laptop toward his side of the room. "We're doing great. Myra shared with us how she was able to see your vision. That was freaky."

"Yeah, I know, we're going to give Commander Irons a call after we're finished chatting to see if anyone turned up at the morgue recently. So far, my visions have been matching with bodies being found."

Myra's bright red earrings jiggled as she spoke. "Be sure to find out if the young woman had a certain station in life. I feel as if she was either a high ranking official or related to one."

"I'll be sure to ask." Marie tilted the laptop back. "Mimi, how is Bailey doing? I really miss him."

Mimi chuckled. "He's doing fine. He's sleeping right now. I just brought him in from a walk."

Gale shifted the laptop toward her. "Where's Harry?"

"He had a meeting with one of his students this morning. But he did give me some information to pass on. There's quite a bit here, so give me a minute to organize his writing." Mimi opened the small notebook and set it on the table.

Gale rolled her eyes. "Of course there is, there always is a lot of information when Harry's involved."

Marie elbowed Gale. "Remember what I said earlier."

Mimi cleared her throat. "Okay, he says here that first psychologists have documented the connection between occult involvement and psychological and emotional disorders. Those involved in the occult spend numerous hours studying and playing games involving conjuring up demons, sacrificing creatures in satanic rituals, and casting spells to disable and kill their enemies, which can affect a person's mental and emotional state, as well as their spiritual beliefs."

"Gee, that sounds encouraging. There's nothing like dealing with spirits and then adding a twist of insanity." Tim got up from the sofa and began eating from the food cart that just arrived.

"He goes on to say the second issue is a danger of spirit possession, which comes from practicing the occult requiring one to empty their mind. Such as, when one uses the Ouija board, they are asked to empty their mind and allow other forces to guide them as they attempt to attain messages. Or other games that require calling upon a spirit to guide them. These practices can open the door for spirit possession."

Marie looked at Gale with concern. "Didn't I tell you messing around with voodoo dolls, and Ouija boards were dangerous?"

Mimi continued, "And thirdly, he mentions about the dangers of violence to oneself and others. I'm having a hard time reading this, but he goes on to state that certain cases involving occultists. One final note he has here is that we must tread lightly when dealing with others who are practicing the occult. There are certain types of hierarchy, and the higher up the chain you go, the more powerful they are."

Myra moved in view of the camera with worried eyes. "Marie, dear, I have been charting your path since your first vision. I need you to be ever so careful. You must promise me to keep your crystals with you, as well as repeating a protection prayer before you all begin your day."

"Oh, I will Myra, I promise. With these new visions and the feelings I've gotten from them, I know this is bigger and more evil than I've ever had to deal with." Marie smiled. "We had a great investigation last night, and we're going to be meeting Thursday to go over the evidence. We had some great personal experiences, and I think we have some strong evidence as well. We'll keep you posted on the findings."

Cory looked at his watch. "I think it's time we had some brunch, considering its eleven o'clock. I want to call Jesse too."

"Yeah, I think we'd better go. Thanks again, everyone for getting together to do this. I'll be sure to keep you in the loop with what we learn at the police department, as well as our investigation findings." Marie drew the hair from her face and draped it behind her ear. "Mimi, thanks again for taking care of the house and Bailey. Myra, thanks for helping me stay grounded and protected. I'm going to adhere to all of yours and Harry's advice."

The group replied in unison, "You're welcome. We'll talk to you soon."

Marie logged off and closed the laptop. "Hey Tim, make sure you save some of that food for us, okay? You look like a crazed lunatic on an eating frenzy."

"Sorry, it smells so good, and I'm starving."

Gale joined in and grabbed a sausage link. "This is delicious. Tim, Marie's right, slow down. You're going to explode here in a minute."

Cory grabbed his cell phone. "I'm going to call Jesse now. Marie, can you grab me some juice, please. I'll see if Jesse can meet with us, and then I'll join in on the chow fest."

Marie laughed. "Well, I'm going for a swim first, and then I'm eating. If I tried to eat now, I'd sink to the bottom of the pool."

"Sounds like a plan. I'll bring something to you at the pool when I'm finished." Cory ran his thumb over her cheek. "Hey, and be careful, please. We never seem to know when a vision is going to take over, and I don't need you losing your grip while you're in the pool."

"I will, I promise. See you in a bit." Marie grabbed her robe and walked toward the bathroom to change.

Gale grabbed Marie's elbow. "Cory's right, please try to be as in tune as you can while you're swimming. This stuff makes me nervous when you're not in control. I'm not used to that."

"Aw gee, girlfriend, I've never seen you vulnerable before." Marie's smile disappeared when Gale didn't smile back. "Don't worry. I'm fine. And I'll be extra in tune, as you call it, the entire time. I promise."

Gale smiled. "Thanks, because I need you around to keep buying antiques from me, ya know?"

Marie shook her head and went into the bathroom to change into her bathing suit and yelled out from behind the door. "I knew you had an ulterior motive."

Cory rapped on the door. "You're going to have to eat now and forget the swim."

Marie poked her head out from behind the door. "Why?"

"Because I just got off the phone with Jesse and there weren't any bodies found yesterday. He double-checked, but no one came in."

Marie cinched her robe tight and came out of the bathroom. "Really? I would have thought a young woman would have been brought in. My visions have been spot-on."

"Maybe they just haven't found her yet." Tim popped a piece of bacon into his mouth.

"Hey yeah, that may be it, maybe they just haven't found her yet." Gale sat down next to Tim and yanked a sausage out of his hand. "You need to slow down and save some food for the rest of us, okay?"

"Either way, Jesse said for us to meet him at his office

within the hour." Cory looked at Marie. "He wants you to sit down with the sketch artist again."

Marie plopped down into the chair and grabbed a pancake off of the platter. "Wow, okay, I certainly wasn't expecting a no-show on the body. Well, it looks like I'll have to postpone my swim. And man, these pancakes are amazing."

"I know, and if I keep eating them, I'm going to have to join you in that swim." Gale grabbed another sausage link out of Tim's hand.

"Alright, let me shower, and then I guess we'll be off." Marie took a quick sip of juice and headed back to the bathroom.

As the hot water hit Marie's face, she couldn't help but wonder what was off with her vision. She also felt guilty for being disappointed that a body hadn't been found. After all, that would be good news, but it still left her frustrated with this newfound ability and not being able to foresee the answers. She had to agree with Gale. She didn't like not being in control.

NINE

Jesse stared at the sketch pad and carefully eyed Marie. "So, this is the latest vision you had?"

"Yes, it is. This one was a bit creepier. Not that the others weren't, but I saw her in what looked like a mausoleum. There were candles all around a crypt or tomb. And then there was a pentagram painted on a stone wall." Marie got nervous from Jesse's stare. "You look like you don't believe me."

"Oh, I believe you. And you said there were slash marks on her body as if they were made from a knife, right? Can you remember where exactly these slashes were?"

Marie sat back in her chair. "Well, I seem to remember one on her left thigh. I saw blood on her stomach area so I would assume there as well. Oh, and there were a few on her right forearm. Is that significant?"

Cory looked at Jesse and leaned on the arm of his chair. "What is it, Jesse? What are you thinking, and why are the knife slashes so important?"

Jesse removed his glasses and rubbed his eyes for a moment and slipped them back on his face. "Because this sketch of yours is from one of the women from that cold case. She had slash cuts on her stomach and thighs, and up and down on her arms."

Marie sat up straight in her chair. "How can you tell it's the same woman? You said those bodies had floated from all over after Katrina hit."

"Yes, well, this body stayed in the mausoleum. The cemetery we found her in had flooded. After many bodies were scattered, one of the groundskeepers of the cemetery began to go through to make sure no bodies were missing. Upon entering this particular crypt, he found her still strapped on top. The water had distorted and bloated the body, but I'm confident this is the same woman. Especially with this scarf tied around her neck. What color was it, by the way?"

Marie's eyes got wide. "Oh my, I completely forgot about the scarf... it was red with those diamonds in the design. I mean, I remember seeing it, but I forgot I had the sketch artist draw it."

"Well, I distinctly remember recovering this woman myself." Jesse set the sketch pad down and stood up from his chair. "You see, this was the former Governor's daughter, Elizabeth. She was only seventeen years old. My partner and I had to inform the Governor ourselves. It was probably one of the worst days of my career as an officer. I know the family very well. I was engaged to her older sister Monica."

"Was? What happened?" Marie grabbed Cory's hand and held it tight.

"I don't know. The family slowly fell apart. They withdrew themselves from the public. The Governor resigned shortly after that. Monica was depressed, and I couldn't snap her out of it, no matter how I tried to help her. Eventually, she broke off the engagement, and the family moved to Texas." Jesse walked over to the office window and stared out into the street. "I was like a caged animal when she broke it off. I became obsessed with the case. And when we were unable to find any of the murderers, well I guess it's never really left me."

"There's nothing worse than an unsolved case, but when you add that whole scenario on top of it, it makes it personal." Cory rubbed Marie's hand with his thumb.

Marie uncrossed her legs. "I'm so sorry this is drudging up old wounds for you, Commander. I was sure it was a vision of a recent murder. I'm a little confused as to why I saw this vision now. The last two were recent victims you found. Speaking of which, were you able to identify the second woman who had the baby?"

Jesse turned from the window and sat down. "Yes, it was a woman from Arkansas. Her name was Laura Faye Johnson. Her parents are flying in to confirm her identity. They never even knew she was pregnant."

"Tim told us that sometimes an occult would bring women into the group and impregnate them just to sacrifice the baby." Marie shuddered.

"Yes, well, that is true, but we haven't found any remains of a baby anywhere. We'll continue to search for one, but there are a lot of crazed women who steal babies because they're unable to conceive on their own."

"That's terrible. I never heard of such a thing." Marie stood up and waved for Gale and Tim to come into the office.

Gale walked in and sat down next to Marie at the conference table. "So, did you find out who the woman was?"

"Yes, we did. It's a cold case that Commander Irons was working on." Marie pulled a bottle of water from her purse and opened it. "She was the daughter of the former Governor who was in office during Katrina."

"The Governor's daughter, didn't Myra say she felt like the

woman was influential or related to someone who was?" Gale looked at Marie wide-eyed and then looked at Jesse.

"Oh, that's right. I forgot about that." Marie looked at Jesse. "I don't know if that has any significance, but Myra, my mentor I told you about, dreamt about my vision last night while we were doing our investigation. She picked up on the fact that the woman had an influential position or was tied in with someone who was. It seems to fit this cold case as well."

"There's no doubt your visions are correct about accuracy. I think I know why your visions are crossing from the past to the present." Jesse leaned back in his chair.

Cory asked, "Which is?"

"As I said the other day... I think the perpetrators are starting all over again. I'm not sure why they stopped, or if they ever left New Orleans. But I refuse to let this crime go unsolved." Jesse looked at Cory. "As you said, there's nothing worse than an unsolved case."

"I need to try and refocus and meditate a little more. There has to be something I'm missing between all of these visions. I need some help as to what they all have in common." Marie looked at Gale. "Do you think Delia would help me?"

"Gee, I don't know. I mean, she said she would. And I think she's been a psychic long enough to have the ability to help."

Jesse looked at Tim and Cory. "Do you think both of you could give me some time today? I was hoping to have some new eyes on the old case files."

"Yeah, we'd be glad to help." Cory looked at Marie. "Is that okay with you?"

"Sure, I think I'm going to see if Madame Boisseau is available for some consultation." Marie stood up and put her hand out to Jesse. "Thanks again for not thinking I'm a nut. If there's anything else that happens, I'll be sure to let you know."

Jesse smiled and shook Marie's hand. "Not a problem, and I've lived in this city long enough to know that just because you can't always explain something, doesn't mean it isn't true. As I said, I'm a man of science and facts when it comes to solving a case. But I've also solved a lot of crimes with my cop intuition. And my gut tells me you're going to help us solve this case, once and for all."

"I hope so and thank you for the vote of confidence. I think you have more faith in me than I do." Marie chuckled.

Tim asked, "Do you have any suggestions for a good place to eat?"

"I'd suggest the Bistro on Dauphine Street. It's got some great pub grub. It has a little for everyone. There are traditional Creole dishes and some not so traditional entrées. They have a great wine list to choose from as well." Jesse looked at Cory. "I may join you if you don't mind."

"That works." Cory leaned over and kissed Marie on the cheek. "Now be careful with Madame Delia, okay? Gale, make sure you're with her during all of this. I prefer someone to be around when she's delving into her unknown abilities."

Gale nodded. "Will do."

Tim looked at Gale. "Stay in touch, and we'll meet you all, say around, six-thirty?"

"Six-thirty, it is." Gale winked and followed Marie out of the office.

THE SUN CAST a glow on Delia's copper skin through the stained glass windows. Her head wrap was the color of bronze and teal and matched her koto dress. The heavy global earrings hung low off her ears, as the countless number of gold bracelets jingled when she moved her arms. Her lipstick was darker than her skin, and her nail polish was a bright red. The incense burned slow, and the smoke twirled up and feathered out through the room.

Delia's eyes remained closed as she breathed in deep and then spoke quietly into the room. "Father-Mother God, I ask dat I be cleared and cleansed within da universal white Christ light, da green healing light and da purple transmuting flame. Within God's will and for my highest good I ask dat any and all negativity and evil be completely sealed in its own light, captured within da ultraviolet light, cut off and removed from me. Impersonally, with neither love nor hate, I return all negativity and evil to its source of emanation, decreeing dat it never again be allowed to re-establish itself within me or anyone else in any form. I now ask dat I be placed within a triple capsule of da universal white Christ light of protection, and for dis blessing, I give thanks."

She opened her eyes and gazed at Marie. "We are protected. I feel your third eye is open and clear. What would ya like to know?"

Marie slowly took a deep breath and released it. "I would like to know why my latest visions are involving these women who were murdered through these satanic rituals. And why they are crossing over from the past with the present."

Delia continued to stare into Marie's eyes. "Ya vibration is powerful, and spirit can pick up on dis. From da moment of ya touching da phone in ya hotel is when da vibrations connected with ya third eye. Ya more open than ya realize. And a very willing aide for dese lost souls to tap into, which is why ya must be careful because dey is leading ya into their memory of what happened to dem. It will pull ya into da evil of da occult. Dere are many sides of voodoo and da occult, but what dey have experienced is evil."

"Is there any way you can see who has been murdering these poor women?"

"No, chile, if I could do dat, I'd be a millionaire." Delia's laugh shook the table beneath her. "But dese souls are unsettled. Dat's why they are comin' to ya. Dey needs to be put to rest, and dey won't be able to until dere story is told."

"Is there anything I need to know, or anyone I need to watch out for?" Marie uneasily shifted in her chair.

"As long as ya can keep ya mind and third eye clear, ya be alright. Ya spirit guides are with ya."

"I don't see them all of the time. Why do I see them more when I'm in danger?" Marie frowned and threw up her hands.

"Because dat's the way dey want to appear to ya for now. But as ya get better at meditating, ya will see dem plain enough." Delia relaxed her shoulders and slumped back into her chair. "Dat's all I have for now. Ya seem to have drained me. Ya more powerful than ya think, chile."

Marie smiled. "That's what Myra always says too."

Gale crossed her legs. "I have a question. Why can't Marie see what's going to happen to her?"

Delia smiled. "Because it's easy to see someone else's fate, then ya own. Dat's just da way of a psychic. We can't read ourselves."

"I see, well, can you give me a reading?" Gale sat up in the chair and set her hands on her thighs. Her carbon hair rippled down over her shoulders. Her emerald sweater hugged her hips over her classic washed jeans. She batted her heavily applied mascara eyelashes and pressed her brightly painted red lips together.

Delia removed a deck of tarot cards from a felt cloth and laid them out on the table. She began to shuffle them from the end and then handed the deck to Gale. "Please hold da deck for a minute and then set dem on da table."

Gale did as she was instructed and placed them in the middle of the table. "I've never had a tarot card reading before."

Delia touched the deck for a few seconds and then spread the deck across the table in an arc. "Please pick three cards from da deck and keep dem face down."

Gale randomly chose three cards and set them in front of the deck. "Okay, I guess I'm ready for this."

Delia lined the cards up beside each other. She turned over the first card called The Chariot. "Dis card is facing upright toward ya which means dat ya are very ambitious in achieving ya goals. Ya have worked to build up a successful existence."

She turned the second card over called The Star. "With dis card, upright and facing ya means dere will be fresh hope and healing of old wounds. Ya have strong influences over others, and ya have a lot of confidence."

Gale giggled. "I don't know about any old wounds, but I've always had a lot of confidence. Not sure about the influence over anyone, though."

Marie purposely coughed. "You don't think you have any influence over Tim?"

Gale scrunched up her nose. "Oh, be quiet. Let Delia continue."

Delia flipped the third card. "Oh, dis seems to fit ya."

Gale stared at the card called 'The High Priestess' facing upside down. "What does that mean? And why is this one upside down?"

Marie placed her hand on Gale's arm. "Sit still, would you? Let Delia continue."

Delia looked at Marie and then at Gale. "Dis card facing upside down means a lack of foresight with superficial knowledge. Ya tend to be ignorant of facts and feelin's. It also means in women, an inability to come to terms with other women or demselves. Things and circumstances are not what they seem."

"I'm not superficial. I can deal with other women and their feelings."

"I think ya need to be sure ya have all da facts of a situation. Don't go jumpin' into somethin' ya don't know anythin' about. Ya may think dat ya know somethin' about another person, but things may not be as they seem." Delia put all of the cards back in the deck.

"I always thought I read people pretty well, don't you think so, Marie?" Gale sat back and folded her arms against her chest.

Marie rolled her eyes. "Oh, let's see, you give Harry a hard time for no reason, other than according to you he's a geek. You've been giving Brigitte a hard time because she smiled at Tim in the wrong way. So, you being ignorant of facts and feelings seem to fit you perfectly."

Gales sat straight up in her chair. "Harry shows off with all of his so-called expertise in everything. I can't stand a show-off. And Brigitte, well she did flirt with Tim, and she's always correcting my attire."

Marie's eyebrows went up. "Correcting your attire? All she said was the six-inch heels you wore to the investigation were a little out of place when you're crawling around setting up equipment and walking around for hours doing an investigation."

"Yeah well... so, she wears her tops too tight."

"Okay, I have no idea what that has to do with anything, but Gale come on, you know you can be pretty dramatic, and you tend to make quick assumptions about people you haven't given a chance to get to know." Marie winked.

"I don't agree with you, and I don't think I influence Tim." Gale stood up and grabbed her purse.

Delia's chest bounced as she laughed at Marie and Gale. "I can see how da two of ya are such good friends. Ya both are the yin and the yang. Marie, ya make sure ya keep ya third eye clear, remember how powerful it can be. And if ya both don't mind, I'd like to clear all of da negative spirits dat can try and break da circle of light when I give a reading."

Delia chanted a prayer and waved smoke from the burning sage toward Marie and Gale. She explained how sage cleared any unwanted negativity and then began to gather herbs, roots, and oils and mixed them while chanting another prayer. She placed the ingredients into two soft red cloth bags and tied the end with a small string made of jute.

Delia handed the bags to Marie and Gale. "Dis is gris-gris. Keep it wit ya at all times. It will bring ya good luck and protect ya from evil. Dere has been many meanings of the gris-gris, but I only use it for protection."

Marie and Gale took the bags and placed them in their purses. They thanked Delia for her insight and protection. They promised to stay in touch and Marie assured her she would focus on her meditation and keeping her third eye clear, even though she wasn't feeling particularly strong in that department. It had become increasingly frustrating trying to help assist in solving who was maliciously murdering these poor women and still learning to deal with her ability.

TEN

GALE POINTED TOWARD CORY, Tim, and Jesse standing under the red canopy of the Bistro and waved. "Marie, there they are. Let's not jump right in with what Delia just told us. I'm not real thrilled with some of the things she said about me."

Marie replied, "Sure, that's fine. It's never easy learning things about yourself, especially if you don't agree with them."

Gale smirked and rolled her eyes. "Gee, thanks."

Marie chuckled and crossed the street toward Cory. "Hey, you weren't waiting here long, were you?"

Cory smiled and wrapped his arm around Marie's waist. "No, just a few minutes. The place is pretty busy, but Jesse got us a table."

"That's great because I'm starving." Gale grabbed Tim's hand and pulled him close to her. "So how was your afternoon reading through case files?"

"Well, I think we learned a great deal. We can share it with you once we sit down." Tim opened the door of the main entrance. "How about you two, did Madame Delia help you out with anything?"

Gale quickly glanced at Marie and then smiled at Tim. "Why don't we all wait until we get some food ordered? I need a margarita."

Marie looked at the décor of the bistro and saw how plain and physically unattractive it was in comparison to Napoleon House. If it weren't for the mirrors on the walls, it would almost feel claustrophobic. In fact, if it weren't for the canopy on the outside, she wouldn't have thought it was even a place to dine.

Jesse took the menu the server handed him and looked at Cory. "I highly recommend the chicken Creole with andouille and Creole tomato sauce. It's very good."

Gale wrinkled her nose. "What is that?"

Jesse chuckled. "It's a spicy smoked pork sausage. The entire dish is quite zesty but excellent."

Tim perused the menu and took a sip of ice water. "This gumbo du jour sounds good."

Gale shook her head. "Why don't you try something different? I mean, come on, you've had enough gumbo to last you a lifetime."

Cory chuckled and placed his hand on Marie's thigh. "What looks good to you?"

"I think I'll try this bistro salad. I'm in the mood for some shrimp." Marie placed the menu on the table and put the cloth napkin on her lap. "I'm surprised this place has cloth napkins. It's not much to look at in here, is it?"

Jesse replied, "No, it's not a fancy place, but the food far outweighs the décor."

Marie handed her menu to the slightly stout server with auburn hair and piercing blue eyes. "Thank you, and I'd like a margarita as well. So, Jesse, were you guys able to link anything between the cases?"

Jesse leaned forward and set his elbows on the table. "Yes, we did. But first, I wanted to share with you the findings from the medical examiner's report on the woman who was murdered for her baby. There were no findings to back up it was an occult related death. No distinguishing marks were found on her body that would indicate she had been abused sexually or otherwise. Plus, we haven't found any corpses of a baby to this point. It looks as though this was just another random act of violence for the woman's baby. As I said earlier, there are a lot of sick, crazed women out there who will go to desperate lengths to have a child."

Marie shook her head. "Okay, I'm not quite sure why I picked up on this woman. Is anyone doing anything to find the child?"

"Yes, we have some men on it. But until something proves this act of violence was a part of a satanic ritual, we're going to set this one aside so we can concentrate on what's relevant." Jesse took the glass of beer from the server and gulped it half down and set it on the table. "Wow, I really needed that."

"Okay, then what else did you learn looking through the old cases?" Gale took a sip of her margarita and closed her eyes and sighed.

Cory replied, "That it gets more confusing as we read through them and try to match it with these latest victims. There are some similarities, but then on further review, something throws a monkey wrench into the findings."

"Can you give us some examples?" Marie took a sip of her margarita and bit into a green fried tomato.

Cory continued, "Most of the cold cases had findings of malicious physical abuse that would normally point toward them being murdered in a satanic ritual. Such as the skinning that Jesse spoke of before and the toxic screenings showed mind-altering drugs like Ritalin, cannabis, hashish, or even cocaine. These latest victims showed no signs of either."

Jesse took another sip of his beer. "Now that can mean two

things that neither of these latest victims had anything to do with an occult related death. Or the offenders have grown wiser and are using other means to cover their trails."

"It sounds as if this is a dead end." Gale finished her margarita and waved at the server to order another.

"Yeah, well, it wasn't the most productive afternoon." Cory looked at Jesse. "I can see why this has haunted you for so long. There has to be something we're missing, something that isn't showing up in the files."

Marie watched Tim stuff an entire piece of toasted ravioli into his mouth and chuckled. "Has anyone interviewed the families? Maybe they suspected there were changes in the behavior of these women."

Jesse stopped in mid gulp and set his beer down. "We hadn't had the chance to interview the families. Frankly, we didn't think any of these women were related to the occult. I think we're going to readdress the type of questions we need to ask the family members. Marie, would you be willing to be a part of the interviews?"

"Me... why? What would I be able to do?"

"I think you may have a little insight. Possibly pick up on anything that we can't."

"I've never actually used my ability in that manner, but I'm open to just about anything now. Delia helped me with some techniques of meditation that should guide me a little better than what I've been able to do."

"Speaking of Delia, how'd your readings go?" Tim smiled when the server placed his plate of gumbo in front of him.

Gale tried to focus her eyes on the margarita and talked into the glass. "Oh... this and that."

Cory frowned. "What, I can't hear you."

Marie sighed. "Okay, we might as well tell you, we've been trying to keep the conversation from it, but she didn't have any real answers as to why the past and present victims are reaching out to me other than I'm a beacon."

Cory grabbed Marie's hand. "And?"

"And, well, it's just a matter of me keeping my third eye clear and meditating."

"Okay, I know you well enough. There's something else you're not telling us." Cory looked Marie straight in the eye.

Gale blurted out and almost choked on her margarita. "Tim, do I influence you to do things you normally wouldn't do?"

Tim's brow went straight up. "You influence me? Why would you ask that?"

"Because Madame Delia said I had a lot of confidence, which I'm aware of, and that there will be a healing of old wounds, which I have no idea what that means. But then she said I influenced someone. Marie seems to think I influence you." Gale pouted.

Tim stopped chewing and smiled. "Gale, no, I don't think you influence me... completely, and maybe the healing of old wounds has to do with that whole argument going on between your sister and aunt."

"Oh yeah, that's right. Maybe they're going to make up finally."

Marie finished her margarita. "Delia did have some interesting information for Gale on one of the tarot cards. The first two cards were very positive. They were the chariot and star, which was spot-on to Gale's personality. But the third card was the high priestess which I think hit the nail on the head about Gale, but she doesn't agree with me."

Gale replied, "It may be sort of close to how I am, but not completely."

"Is someone going to fill us in on what the high priestess card means?" Cory set his fork down and looked at Marie.

"It just basically means that Gale is superficial and jumps to conclusions about people and situations." Marie shifted back away from Gale's flying hand.

"She also said things aren't always as they seem." Gale finished her margarita and frowned at Marie. "She also gave us some gris-gris bags."

"Gris-gris bags, what the hell are gris-gris bags?" Tim blew on his steaming spoonful of food.

"They're made up of herbs, oils, and roots. She said another protection prayer over the bags as she created them." Marie pulled out her bag and showed everyone.

"I've heard of those. I never really believed in any of that voodoo stuff. Do you believe the reading she gave you?" Jesse took a bite of his chicken creole.

Gale shrugged her shoulders and then looked at Tim. "I guess I do, as I start to think about what she said, it does reflect my personality."

"You are a very confident woman, which is what attracted me to you, to begin with. But because of that confidence, you don't always gather all of your facts about a situation or person, and you dive right into a scenario... good, bad, or otherwise. I've always told you to learn more about a situation before you jump to conclusions. One of these days, someone is going to retaliate to your comments or accusations, and you may not be prepared on how to handle them." Tim leaned over and kissed Gale on the cheek.

"I'd say it's been quite an interesting afternoon for all of us." Jesse looked at Marie. "Can you be available to meet with some of the family members of these victims? They're coming to the precinct to sign some paperwork to release the bodies. We didn't feel it was necessary to hold them, but if you're able to pick up on anything, that would be helpful."

"Yeah, I can help you with that." Marie looked at Cory. "I'd also like to call Myra when we get back to the hotel this evening. When I have too much rolling around in my head, she's usually the one who can help me process everything."

Cory placed his hand on Marie's thigh and nodded. "Why don't we finish our dinners and maybe take a walk around the French Quarter. I'd like to maybe stroll down Bourbon Street."

Jesse shook his head. "I'm going to pass on that one. I've had enough experiences to last me a lifetime from there. Just watch your pockets and purses. We have at least ten pickpocket cases a night."

"Good advice, we'll be sure to keep an eye out." Cory placed his napkin on the table.

"What a great idea, Cory, I was anxious to stroll down Bourbon Street. It'll take my mind off of all of this negative stuff and possibly get me in a more seductive mood." Gale winked at Tim.

"Oh, there's no doubt the sights you'll witness will be more than interesting." Jesse laughed and stopped Cory from paying the bill. "This one is on me. You can pick up the next tab."

"Thanks, Jesse, and we'll stay in touch." Cory helped slip Marie's jacket on. "Alright everyone, it looks as though we're headed to Bourbon Street."

"Great, I'm ready for some live music." Marie followed Cory's gesture and walked in front of him.

Tim held the door open for everyone. "We're only a block away according to this street map."

They turned the corner onto Bourbon Street and immediately heard a mixture of live music and saw a line of lit neon advertising signs on every business front. Hordes of people walked along the sidewalk and in the middle of the road carrying opened cans and glasses of alcohol. There were souvenir shops, restaurants, bars with take-out windows for liquor, and voodoo shops. It looked like one big carnival that was open twenty-four seven.

Gale pointed to the men standing on an upstairs balcony. "Check those guys out... they're having a great time."

Tim quickly maneuvered and caught a string of beads that were tossed down toward Gale. "I suspect they want you to respond in kind and lift your shirt, but I believe I'm going to have to ask you to keep those for me."

Gale laughed and wrapped her arms around Tim's waist. "Absolutely, I'm keeping these puppies under wraps."

Cory stopped in front of the opened doors of the Tropical Isle. "Now this group is good. It sounds like Zydeco music."

Marie smiled and walked through the entrance. "Check out the washboard player. He's grabbing people out of their chairs to dance."

Gale nodded her head to the right. "There's a table over there against the wall. Let's grab it before someone else does."

Marie hung her purse on the back of the stool and glanced out into the street. "Gale, check out the guy wearing the gold sequence bra and green tulle skirt. He looks like a ballerina gone bad."

"Oh wow, now that takes some serious nerve... or drinking some serious gallons of beer."

They spent the rest of the evening listening to live music up and down Bourbon Street and digesting all of the sites the town had to offer. There was no doubt in Marie's mind they had finally submerged themselves into the wild side of the French Quarter.

JIMMY CAMBRAY LAUGHED and ran as fast as he could from the group. His shoulder length brown hair flew back away from his face as his tall, lean frame continued the fast pace.

He knew his older brother Kevin would whip the tar out of him if he caught up to him. I only wanted to hang out with Kevin and be a part of the gang. How was I supposed to know I would catch them in the middle of some stupid drinking game?

He continued to run into City Park parallel to the wetlands. As he looked back to see how close they were, he tripped and fell and twisted his ankle. He yelled out in pain and rolled over to see what it was that caught his foot. Halfway buried in the ground was a small, charred skull and other tinier bones. When he realized it looked to be human, he let out a scream that echoed through the park.

Cory watched Gale and Tim devour the breakfast cart like two mad dogs on a carcass. "You two seem to be extremely hungry. Did Bourbon Street bring out the animal in you?"

Gale stuffed a beignet in her mouth. "Oh yeah, wasn't that amazing? I mean it was just unbelievable what goes on. It got me in the mood if you know what I mean."

"I think he gets the picture." Tim smiled at Gale and popped an entire piece of bacon into his mouth. "I'm surprised Marie is still sleeping."

"Yeah, she had a late night talking with Myra and her folks."

"Oh, how'd that go? Did she find out how that little boy spirit is related?" Gale took a sip of mimosa and sighed. "Wow, now that's good."

"I don't know. I fell asleep before she came back to bed. Normally chatting with Myra helps her to relax, so I'm glad she's still sleeping." Cory took a bite of a crawfish pie. "Gale, she felt bad teasing you about Delia's reading. She didn't mean for it to come off as criticism."

"I know, and I didn't take it that way. It's hard for me to admit my faults... and when she's right."

"Boy, you people sure do eat loud." Marie walked out from the bedroom and sat on Cory's lap. "Good morning, I missed rolling over and finding you there."

Cory kissed Marie's neck. "I hated leaving you there, but I knew you needed the rest. Would you like some coffee?"

"Yes, please, and thank you. To answer your question, Myra did help me to focus again. Just as she always does. Gale, she gave me some building tools for my meditation and said she's going to try and meditate on all of this as well. She'll keep me posted on what she envisions." Marie took the cup Cory gave her and blew on the steaming coffee. "Ah, the best part of the morning."

"You don't really mean that, do you?" Cory grinned wide.

"No, of course not, coffee comes in second after you." Marie winked.

"Okay, you two." Gale drained the last drop of mimosa. "What did your parents tell you about the little boy spirit?"

Marie pulled her hair away from her face and rubbed her eyes. "Well, you're never going to believe this story. Ludomir, who is the little boy spirit, is on my mother's side of the family. I figured it was French. Anyway, my mother said the story in the family was that Ludomir was around the age of nine in the early seventeen nineties during the French revolution. He was guillotined, along with many other children because their families were suspected as traitors. It was said his sister escaped and went into hiding. The legend in my family stated Ludomir came back and protected his sister in spirit, which is why she was able to escape."

"Guillotined? Why that's horrible. Who could ever do that to anyone, let alone children?" Gale shook her head and pushed her plate of food away in disgust.

"Yeah, I agree. Ludomir is my fourth great uncle, I think. It was hard to follow the ancestry that my mother explained, and it was so late. Apparently, he has come back in spirit to protect and guide me as well."

"Wow, how cool is that? I wonder if I have any guardian angels." Gale stood up and stretched her back.

"We all do according to Myra. Some of us have more than one or two." Marie walked over to the breakfast cart and spooned some eggs onto a plate. "Wow, how much did you all eat? There's hardly anything left over here."

"Yeah, sorry. We worked up an appetite." Tim shrugged and jammed his hands in his pockets.

Marie heard Cory's cell phone vibrating on the desk and read the name on the screen. "It looks like Jesse's calling you. Why do I have a feeling this isn't good news?"

Cory answered the phone and put it on speaker. "Jesse, how are you? I have you on speaker so everyone can hear you. What's up?"

Jesse's voice echoed through the cell phone. "Hello everyone, I hope you all enjoyed Bourbon Street. Cory, I'm afraid I'm going to need you and Marie to come back down to the station. It looks as though Marie's vision matches up with the pregnant woman who was murdered in a possible satanic ritual."

Marie sat up in her chair and leaned toward the cell phone. "Did someone find the baby?"

"Why don't you come down to the station and we can discuss it then. I'd rather not talk about it over the phone."

"Okay, we have an analysis meeting with André and the group for lunch. We can try and squeeze in a stop there on our way." Marie took the last bite of eggs and gulped down her coffee.

"That's fine. I'll see you within the hour."

"Sounds good Jesse, see you soon." Cory hit the end button and looked at Marie. "You were right, it wasn't good news, except for the fact that it may finally match up with your vision. What could have possibly transpired overnight?"

"I don't know, but I'm certainly anxious to get down there." Marie looked at Gale. "Can you contact André and let him know Cory and I may be a few minutes late? You and Tim go on over and help with the analysis. We'll be there as soon as we can."

"I guess so, although I would rather go with you and Cory to the station."

"I know, but Philippe said they need all the help they can get on going through all of the evidence. I promise to give you all of the details of what we learn." Marie draped her arm around Gale's shoulders. "You promise me to keep your gris-gris with you, okay? With all that's been going on, it's a good feeling having a little extra protection."

ELEVEN

Marie's stomach churned when Jesse laid the photographs of the charred tiny skull and bones on his desk. "Oh my gosh, that's horrible. Are you sure these are the bones from an infant, and they're a match to the woman I saw in my vision?"

"Yes, you can see how the skull has many structural elements that fuse together into solid bone as growth develops, such as the frontal bone. These regions are very fibrous and moveable, which is necessary for birth and later growth. You can also see where the vertebral column consists of five bones which normally are separated at birth and fuse together into a solid structure in later years. This cartilage between the segments of bone allows further growth. I also urged them to run a forensic DNA test from the skin remains of the bones, and the woman vic in your vision. The DNA is a match." Jesse flipped the photographs over and slipped them into a manila folder.

"So, we are dealing with the occult, and it does look as though my visions are lining up with the scientific end of things." Marie sat down in a chair and sighed.

Cory sat down next to Marie, and lovingly rubbed her back. "I thought you'd be glad to hear this report. You said you were confused. Weren't you beginning to have some self-doubt?"

"Yes, I was, and I am glad this all corresponds to the forensic reports. But it still doesn't get us any closer to who did this, and I still don't have all of the answers to my visions. I still think they're crossing over each other."

Jesse looked at Cory. "With this latest bit of evidence concurring with Marie's visions and the fact that you're all beginning to get involved, I'm thinking that whoever is responsible for these murders isn't going to like anyone snooping around with the cops. Would you mind if I gave you all some police protection?"

Cory smiled. "I wouldn't say no."

Lost in thought, Marie stood up from her chair and leaned over Jesse's desk. "Do you have any of the belongings to this latest victim, what was her name?"

"Laura Faye Johnson, and yes I do, we won't release any of it to the families now until this case is solved, which by the way I'd still like for you to observe the interview with the family if you don't mind."

"Sure, I don't mind. But what I'd like to do is possibly see some of her effects and test this psychometry on one of her personal items."

Cory raised his right eyebrow. "Do you think that'll work?"

"All I can do is try." Marie rubbed her arms as a chill ran through her.

Jesse picked up the office phone. "Ted, hey, yeah it's Jesse. Would you mind bringing in some of the belongings on Laura Faye Johnson to my office as soon as possible? Yeah, thanks." Jesse hung up the phone. "We can only let you touch a few small items; the forensic team is still examining most of the clothing."

Marie turned and looked out the window. "That's fine. I only need to touch something she would have touched."

Cory walked over and stood behind Marie and began to rub her upper arms. "Are you sure you want to do this? What if I can't bring you back out of a vision?"

Marie turned and looked up into Cory's gorgeous brown eyes. "Don't worry, between you and Jesse and half of the police force here, not to mention my spirit guides. I'll be fine."

A short, portly gentleman with a bad comb-over walked into the office and handed a clear plastic forensic bag filled with a purse, a set of keys, and lipstick to Jesse. "Here are some gloves if you need them."

Jesse smiled and pointed toward Marie. "Thanks, Ted, you can give those gloves to Marie. I have some in my drawer."

Marie smiled at Ted, took the gloves, and began pulling them onto her hands. "Thank you."

Jesse snapped his gloves on and opened the bag. He slowly pulled out the purse and handed it to Marie. "There wasn't much in here. We couldn't find a wallet or any other identification. That was also why we didn't think it matched up to your visions of a satanic ritual. We simply thought they stole her baby and robbed her."

Marie took the purse and sat down in a chair. She closed her eyes, took a few deep breaths, and began rubbing her hands slowly around the bag. Within seconds she saw a quick flash and then a subdued glow of light above her. There was laughter and music in the background, and gradually, Marie saw herself standing in a pub. Laura Faye was sitting at the end of a bar laughing and coyly rubbing her hand along a man's thigh as her belly bulged over her lap. Marie couldn't see the gentleman's face.

The room began to spin, and Marie again saw a quick flash as she felt herself walking and watching Laura Faye and the gentleman stroll through a parking lot. The man leaned her against a car and began groping her breasts and kissing her neck. She laughed, dropping her head back and held onto the man's shoulders. Marie felt herself getting dizzy as she watched Laura Faye swoon and put her hand to her head. Instantly Laura Faye dropped to her knees, and the man picked her up and carried her through the back part of the alley.

There was another quick flash of light, and Marie found herself hazily watching Laura Faye laying under the man screaming and punching her fists into his chest. Out of nowhere, there were droves of people wearing hooded robes circling her and the man as they loudly chanted. Laura continued to scream as the group held her down and tied a gag around her mouth. Marie tried to see the man's face but to no avail, and she slowly began to feel nauseous and dizzy as her eyes began to blur. When they came into focus, the man leaned up wearing a ram's head and plunged a knife into Laura Faye's belly.

Marie heard a scream and realized Cory was patting her cheek and yelling her name. She opened her eyes and found herself clutching the purse while Jesse and Cory knelt in front of her with looks of shock.

Cory grabbed a chair and slid it next to Marie and sat down. "Are you okay?"

"Yes, I'm fine, and I think I saw what happened to Laura Faye." Marie set the purse down on Jesse's desk and began to remove her gloves.

Jesse stood up and sat on the edge of his desk. "I have to say that was one of the strangest things I've encountered in all of my years as a police officer. You were completely out of it and in some sort of a trance. What did you see?"

"Can I please have some water? I always get very fatigued and thirsty after I go through a vision."

"Sure, we have a water cooler just outside the door here. I'll get you one." Jesse walked out for a minute and came back in with a paper cup of water. "Here ya go."

"Thank you." Marie gulped the entire glass of water down and set the cup on the desk. "I saw Laura Faye in a pub somewhere, but I couldn't make out any details of which pub it may have been. It may be a place close to where you found her body. She was sitting at the bar with a man, but I couldn't make out his face. They looked like they knew each other pretty well because they couldn't keep their hands off of each other. Then the next phase of my vision had them kissing like wild animals in a parking lot up against a car. But shortly after that I could feel Laura Faye getting dizzy, and she fell to her knees, and the man carried her to the back part of an alley. Suddenly she was lying on the ground with the man on top of her, and she was screaming and punching him, and then almost instantly there were people dressed in the usual satanic garb chanting and circling the pair of them. The last thing I saw was the man whose face I couldn't make out wearing a ram's head again as he plunged a knife into her belly. Then I heard a scream."

Cory rubbed Marie's arm. "That may have been your scream. You were screaming pretty loud at the end there before you came to."

Jesse rubbed the back of his neck. "Was there anything that stood out for you as to where the pub may have been? Distinguishing pictures on the wall or music playing? She was found on Canal Street. Did you notice any street signs."

"No street signs, I did hear some music, but it wasn't anything unusual, or at least it didn't stand out to me in any way. It looked and sounded like any pub you would walk into anywhere in New Orleans."

"It seems obvious she knew her assailant pretty well. Hard to say if she knew what plans he had for her. As you said earlier, they can brainwash members and impregnate them." Jesse put the purse back into the forensic bag and removed his gloves. "From what you were feeling with being dizzy and nauseous I would suspect she was drugged. But we didn't come up with any toxins in her bloodstream. Her results were below the predetermined cutoff, which gave a negative result for toxins. I'm wondering if we may need to run a more specific and sensitive test."

Marie looked at her watch. "Oh, wow, we're late. We should have been back at the Napoleon House to help with the analysis a half hour ago."

"Yeah, I think you need a little diversion right now." Cory stood up and held Marie's elbow as she got up out of her chair.

Jesse stood up and grabbed the forensic bag. "I'll walk you both out. Marie, I'll give you a call when Laura Faye's family arrives. Cory, I'll get one of my undercover guys to keep a close eye on all of you. I'm also going to take a closer look at some of the pubs around the area where we found Laura Faye. This is a lead we didn't have before, and I'd like you both to stay in touch if you notice anything unusual."

Marie asked, "You mean this hasn't been unusual?"

Jesse chuckled. "Well, anything more unusual than what's taken place so far."

GALE JUMPED in her chair and hit pause on the DVD. "Whoa, you guys need to take a look at this. This was when Marie, Cory, and Katherine were in the dining room, and Madame LaLaurie decided to pay them a visit."

Tim leaned over and looked at the DVD monitor. "Can you pull it over on the big screen?"

Gale saved the data and brought it over to the large monitor. "Okay, I'll take it back a few seconds, but as soon as Marie says Delphine was staring me down with a frown on her face, you'll see the picture fall off the wall."

The group watched from behind, and Philippe jumped when the picture dropped. "Wow, now that looked more like it was whipped off the wall. It didn't just drop."

Katherine asked, "Gale, can you please rewind that and play it back?"

"Sure, I'll slow it down a bit."

"Well, there's no doubt that it didn't slip off the wall. You can see how the bottom of the picture moved out away from the wall first as if it was being picked up and away from the wall."

Brigitte looked at Tim. "And this is where Marie said she saw Delphine staring her down?"

Gale replied before Tim could respond. "Yes, it is. You sound as if you don't believe Marie."

"Don't believe me about what?" Marie entered the room with Cory and walked toward the group standing around Gale.

Gale smiled. "We were looking at the footage of Delphine throwing the picture off the wall. I'm not sure everyone believes you saw her do it."

"Can you play it back for me please?" Marie watched the replay and shrugged her shoulders. "I don't know what to tell you, but Madame LaLaurie was pretty ticked off and threw the picture off the wall. By the way Katherine, was Cassandra very upset?"

"No, she sent it to a local art gallery and had the glass replaced. She wasn't concerned with the cost. She was pretty intrigued as to how it happened. I think this reveal is going to blow her mind."

"Well, Cory and I are sorry we're late. Which equipment is ready for us to review?" Marie placed her sweater on a chair.

André pointed to the chairs next to Gale. "We have some DVD's and recorders there for you to review. The notebooks for each of those are next to the equipment. We've organized all of our notes according to each investigating group and rooms of the house. So far, we've accumulated quite a bit of documentation that backs up most of the claims."

Marie sat down next to Gale and leaned over and whispered in her ear. "Wait until I tell you what just happened at the police station."

"Don't make me wait, tell me now. I've waited long enough."

"Okay, well, the DNA is a match for the woman they found, and the charred baby remains. Oh, Gale, it was horrible. It made my stomach turn when I saw the pictures." Marie shivered remembering the skull and began to share her vision in detail with Gale.

Tim tried to listen to Marie and watch the DVD footage at the same time. "Do you think this will help Jesse out with anything?"

Cory replied, "I think it did. He's going to have his men go to a few of the pubs close to Canal Street where they found Laura Faye. They did a canvas that same day in a few of the local businesses in that area, but now they'll be able to take this information a little further."

Marie felt exhausted and wanted to change the subject. "So, what else have you found from the LaLaurie House?"

"Well, Philippe got an awesome EVP when we were in the room with the pink painted walls." Gale rewound the tape. "Here, put these earphones on and listen right at twelve twenty-three and eighteen seconds."

Marie waited for the tape to hit the time Gale stated and flinched. "Okay, now that was weird. That's amazing. It sounded like it said remove my chains."

"That's exactly what we heard." Tim smiled and turned his monitor toward Marie and Cory. "Now, take a look at this catch. This is you, Cory, and Katherine in the kitchen. Watch when Cory walks past the end of the counter. Look at the chair directly behind him."

"Did that chair just move?" Cory's eyes were wide with shock.

"Yep, it did. Isn't that a great catch? I have to say this investigation has been filled with objects moving." Gale grabbed her earphones and plugged them into her DVD recorder. "We still have a ton of video and audio to review. We'd better get back to it."

André walked over to Marie and Cory. "Before I forget, I'd like to invite you all to my place after the reveal this evening. It's something we usually do after we've given the evidence to the client. Would you all be available around eightish?"

Marie replied, "Sure, that sounds great. We didn't have any plans."

"Good, here's my address. I'll see you all around eight, and we can discuss the investigation and how our client responded to the evidence."

Marie took the piece of paper and slipped it into her pocket. She was glad to have the diversion of reviewing the evidence instead of rehashing those horrible photos of the burned baby in her mind's eye. It felt good to know she was able to use the psychometry to help Jesse with the latest victim, but it still brought on the uncertainty of how well she was able to control these abilities. The only conciliation was she knew her spirit guides would protect her if she lost control and couldn't pull herself out of a vision. One never knew the power of evil when dealing with the occult.

TWELVE

THE BRILLIANT MOON created a glow through the trees upon the marble altar. He stood at the end of the altar between her thighs and held the dagger in his hands, raising it toward the sky, catching the reflection of the moon on her breast. Carefully he whispered his praise and sacrifice for Beelzebub and set the dagger down between her parted thighs as the golden inverted pentagram swung from the chain around his neck.

He raised the chalice in the same fashion and whispered the identical prayer of sacrifice and placed it next to the dagger. The illuminator stood to his left, holding a candle over the bible. The attendant stood next to the illuminator carrying a small gong while the thurifer was at his right, holding a boat of incense.

The congregation of dark-robed and hooded figures stood in their ritual circle as the candle flames danced and swayed in the warm breeze. The gong was struck three times as the deacon and sub-deacon bowed their heads in unison with him.

He raised his hands and chanted aloud, "Before the mighty and ineffable Prince of Darkness and in the presence of the dread demons of the pit, and this assembled company, I acknowledge and confess my past error. Renouncing all past allegiances, I proclaim that Satan-Lucifer rules the earth, and I ratify and renew my promise to recognize and honor Him in all things, without reservation, desiring in return His manifold assistance in the successful completion of my endeavors and the fulfillment of my desires. I call upon you, my Brother, to bear witness and to do likewise."

He removed the black veil from the paten and black wafer and raised it to his chest and gave thanks. He took the thurible and proceeded to incense the altar and the gifts. He saged the chalice and wafer with three counterclockwise strokes and made a profound bow. Then he raised the thurible three times to the inverted cross and bowed. Assisted by the deacon and sub-deacon, he incensed the top of the altar and the sides of the platform. The gong was struck three more times.

He raised his hands again and said, "Therefore, O mighty and terrible Lord of Darkness, we entreat You that You receive and accept this sacrifice, which we offer to You on behalf of this assembled company, upon whom You have set Your mark."

He placed the wafer between her breasts and continued, "In the name of unholy fellowship we praise thee."

She began to feel herself slowly become aware of her surroundings as she heard a low clanging of a gong. The incense burned her nostrils, and her chest felt wet and cold. She sluggishly opened her eyes and saw the glittering stars blink against the dark sky. Suddenly she heard the loud unison chant, and the moon became eclipsed by two hands holding a dagger. When she looked at the nude man wearing a ram's head, she screamed and felt a sharp pain pierce her chest. Blackness set in as the stars began to snuff out one by one slowly.

. . .

GALE FOLLOWED Marie into the antique shop on Royal Street. "Doesn't it bother you when people mock your ability?"

Marie held the door for everyone and smiled. "No, it doesn't. Gale, you forget why I squelched my ability, to begin with. It's okay if someone doesn't believe in my gift. I'm used to it."

Cory grabbed Marie's hand and pulled her close. "Do you realize this is the first time you've called your ability a gift?"

Marie stopped short and looked at Cory. "Wow, really? I hadn't noticed."

"It bugs me for some reason. Brigitte comes across as if she's superior to everyone else and a few of her comments have ticked me off. I mean, you would think being interested in paranormal investigations would give you an open mind, wouldn't you?" Gale peered into a glass case of antique dolls.

"Well, I do agree with having an open mind to be interested in this sort of thing, but she may be more into the scientific part of the investigation. She needs to see proof." Marie winked at Cory. "Cory used to be that way, too until I brought him around."

Cory smiled. "Yes, I was, but I take offense too with some of their questionings. I only get that sort of a read from André and Brigitte. I haven't picked up anyone else. They're noncommittal."

Gale nodded. "Yeah, I agree. Look, I am glad you're getting more comfortable with your gift. I just get a little defensive of the naysayers."

"Maybe that's why you're beginning to develop more of your ability. You seem to be accepting it easier." Tim picked up an antique clock and winced at the price.

Marie smiled, "I never thought of it that way before Tim. You're very intuitive. Did you know that?"

Gale rolled her eyes. "Please, don't pump his ego any more than what it is."

Tim carefully set the clock down and poked Gale's waist. "Let's not get into egos, shall we?"

Cory laughed and pointed to a rosewood game table. "Gale, this would be a nice piece to have in your shop."

Gale picked up the price tag and whistled. "I don't think so. I look for antiques at garage sales or in people's attics. This is a bit out of my price range."

Tim glanced back at Cory and Marie. "Thanks again for dinner, you two, you didn't need to do that."

"Hey, not a problem, thanks for choosing the restaurant. The oysters were fantastic." Cory sized up a French tall case clock and read its detailed history on the label.

"Hey, I think we'd better head over to meet everyone. It's after eight." Gale looped her arm in Tim's and leaned her head on his shoulder.

"Oh yeah, you're right. Let me find André's address. It'll be interesting to hear how everything went." Marie searched through her pockets, looking for the slip of paper.

"I'm looking forward to the reveal, but if anyone starts to make their snide comments again about what you can and can't do, I may just have to slap them." Gale puffed out her heavily endowed chest and marched out of the shop.

Marie chuckled and looked up at Cory. "Why do I get the distinct impression she means Brigitte?"

"MASTER, where should we place the body?" The small-framed beady-eyed man stood with his head bowed, waiting in anticipation.

"In the crypt with the others and be sure you're not followed. We're running out of places to hold our sacrifices until we can destroy them." He removed the ram's head, took the robe from the assistant, and wrapped it around his blood-stained body.

"I think that had to be one of our most successful sacrifices yet. It was a bit out of character, though, no?" She slowly ran her hand up and down his bare chest.

"How do you mean?" He eyed her carefully and motioned for her to walk.

"I thought we were to wait another twenty-eight days until the next full moon. We didn't have our entire congregation with us."

"It needed to be the phase of the waning crescent. We need to be cleansed to rid ourselves of our bad habits. I believe some of the congregation has become too complacent." He wiped the blood from his mouth, and eerily smiled.

"You seem quite pleased with yourself. I believe you enjoyed this sacrifice a little more than usual. You've had your eye on her for quite some time." She looked at him through angered eyes.

"I think you're letting the green-eyed monster rule your thinking and emotions. It has gotten you into trouble in the past. I should think you'd be glad we're rid of her."

"I am in complete control of my emotions. I don't care one way or the other about her. She was loose-tongued and a hindrance. She needed to be taken care of."

"How are your emotions now?" He grabbed her waist and slammed her against a tree. He kissed her mouth hard and bit down on her lip, drawing blood. He began to rip open her robe and savagely groped her breast.

She leaned her head back and smiled up at the moon. "My emotions are at your command."

He stopped short and laughed in her face. "I believe I'm

beginning to tire of you. You're no challenge to me anymore." He lifted his hands from the tree and walked away from her.

She ran the back of her hand across her bloodied lip and whispered. "You shall pay for laughing in my face."

MARIE BALANCED her stance as she held onto the leather strap attached to the bar of the trolley. She read André's address off the slip of paper and then checked the street names labeled on each corner signpost. "I think we get off at the next stop. That should be First Avenue."

"These trolleys sure do need some new shocks. I don't think it would have been any better if we were sitting." Gale leaned against Tim and held onto his arm for support.

"Trolleys, don't have shocks." Tim wrapped his arm around Gale's waist and winked. "It's just metal wheels grinding on metal tracks."

"I'm beginning to realize you know a lot about trivial things. How on earth do you know about trolleys?"

Before Tim could answer, Marie pulled the cord to alert the driver to stop the trolley. "This is First Avenue. Sorry, Tim, I didn't mean to interrupt you, but this is our stop."

Gale held up her hand to stop Tim from answering. "I know, I know, you looked up the history of trolleys before we came here."

Cory chuckled and helped Marie down the steps of the trolley. "I think it's safe to say that we've all learned a great deal about Tim on this trip. Maybe we need to leave the rest of what Tim knows for future travels."

"I guess I like to read about a lot of different things." Tim held onto Gale's elbow as she descended the trolley steps. "And some of the reading is the result of you being pleasantly satisfied all of the time."

Gale's jaw dropped open and then shut. "Okay, let's not get into too many details, but do you mean that thing that you do when..."

"Whoa, I thought you said, let's not get into too many details." Marie stopped on the median and waited for the traffic to clear before crossing the street. "Let's concentrate on finding André's house, shall we?"

They reached the other side of the street and Cory peered over Marie's shoulder to read the slip of paper. "What color is the house, and what street is it on?"

"It's the corner of Fourth and Magazine Street. He says here that it's a Greek revival style home, pale blue with white shutters and large pillars on the porch. The number is eleven forty." Marie spotted the house and pointed. "There it is. Wow, it's beautiful."

"I'll say, check out the gated fence and the garden on the side. Is that a Mercedes parked in the driveway?" Gale rushed up behind Marie and peeked through the wrought iron balusters.

"Yep, that's a Mercedes. Look at the gorgeous brick driveway. It coils around to the back of the house." Marie pushed open the gate and walked toward the steps of the porch.

"Check out the huge gas lighted chandelier hanging from the porch ceiling. The chain must be twenty feet long." Tim looked up in awe at the fixture.

Marie approached the bright red door and rang the antique doorbell. "Okay, this is really cool. It almost sounds like the trolley bell."

André opened the door wearing a heather pin-striped button-down shirt over a plum T-shirt and dark khaki pants. "Hey, you found me. Come on in. We just gathered a few minutes ago. We had a great reveal with Cassandra."

The polished oak floors reflected the light of the overhead

crystal chandelier and gleaned under the plush deep red Persian rug. The stark white walls conveyed a beautiful contrast to the museum oil paintings that hung in unison along the length of the foyer. Potted miniature palm trees sat on the floor while lush ferns lay in the deep windowsills.

"You have a beautiful home. I love all of the foliage here in New Orleans." Marie handed her jacket to André.

"Thank you. I was born in this house. Everything here is the result of my mother's graceful touch. She had the eye for interior design and the flair for what did and didn't work."

"I love the Mercedes parked in the driveway." Gale smiled and stared at an unusual gaudy copper statue of a man and woman entwined with each other. "This has to be French."

Tim rolled his eyes and grabbed Gale's hand. "Let's move along before we offend any more of the man's house, shall we?"

"What, I'm not saying anything that isn't true. Anytime you see something as flamboyant as that. It's typically a French piece. I do have an eye for antiques, remember?" Gale looked at André. "Am I right?"

André chuckled. "Yes, you are. There are quite a few French ornate pieces throughout the house. But what can you say being of French descent and living in New Orleans? Go on into the parlor; the rest of the group is there. Help yourselves to a drink. Philippe makes a mean hurricane."

"Oh, yes, I want to try one of those. It's got all sorts of yummy ingredients." Gale walked through the large doorway into the parlor.

Brigitte was standing next to Philippe, wearing grey low-rise pants with a tight décolleté beige cashmere sweater that accented her breasts. Her hair was neatly tucked behind her ears and fell just at the nape of her neck. Her plump lips left traces of lipstick on the edge of her martini glass.

Gale sneered at Brigitte and whispered in Marie's ear.

"Miss Botox lips is drinking a martini. I pictured here more of a beer drinker."

Marie shook her head and smiled at Philippe. "I hear you make a mean hurricane. I want to try one of those if it's not too much trouble."

Philippe smiled. "It's no trouble at all. I have a pitcher made up already." His white mock turtleneck sat smartly beneath the navy sweater, and his jeans looked neatly starched and pressed.

Cory walked over to the bar and grabbed a bottle of gin and turned to Tim. "I'll make us some martinis. How many olives do you prefer?"

Tim grabbed a glass and sat it next to the vermouth. "I'll take three, please."

Jason puffed on his cigar, holding a glass of bourbon. His business shirt barely covered his gut, which protruded loudly over his belt. "Hello, everyone, glad you could make it. Marie, how are you feeling this evening?"

Marie took a sip of the hurricane and almost choked. "I'm doing well, thank you. And man, this is some concoction. What's in this, anyway?"

Gale sipped her hurricane and said, "I believe I taste some gin and rum, and a little flavor of almond. Oh, and there's some vodka, pineapple, and let me see." She took another sip. "Oh, and I taste grapefruit. How'd I do?"

"Magnifique, that's all of the ingredients. There's a little grenadine syrup and two types of rum, but you managed to taste them all. You have a flair for deciphering a drink." Philippe held up his glass in a toast.

Gale giggled and took another sip. "Why, thank you, Philippe."

Cory handed Tim a drink and faced the group. "Where's Katherine?"

Jason puffed on his cigar as it slouched out the side of his mouth. "She had to meet with one of her artist clients, something about a showing in her gallery."

André entered the room with a glass of scotch. "Yes, Katherine wasn't able to attend the reveal or for drinks with us this evening. She is working on an important showing of one of her new and upcoming artists. Since we all seem to have our drink of choice, I'll get my notes and have Brigitte run the laptop to show you what we shared with Cassandra."

Marie sat next to Cory and Gale on a paisley upholstered settee. The wallpaper had a warm terracotta colored design with green velvet high back chairs and matching drapes. An enormous mirror towered on the wall above the marble fireplace mantel with garland flanking its corners. The live tree in the corner stood at least eight feet tall with stunning traditional ornaments and lights.

The group watched the recorded video André presented to Cassandra and chatted about all of the encounters they had. Marie made mental notes of the equipment she wanted to add to their inventory and commented on how amazing the laser grid scope caught so many apparitions. Tim insisted they get a thermal camera. The conversation came to a lull, and everyone had consumed quite a bit of alcohol.

Brigitte sat next to Tim and glanced over at Marie. "André told me you have been working closely with Commander Irons on some murders that have taken place recently here. Is that true?"

Marie set her drink down and looked at Cory and then back at Brigitte. "Yes, it is. You've already seen some of the articles in the local paper even though Jesse has tried to keep it out of the news."

"Jesse? You know him on a first name basis?" Brigitte got up to make another martini.

Cory replied, "I'm afraid that's due to my relationship with Jesse. He was a guest lecturer at the academy I attended in Charleston."

"So, what brought on this involvement? I mean, how does it tie in with you?" Philippe leaned forward and began stroking his mustache.

"As I explained to you the other night at your meeting, I began having visions that ended up tying in with these murders and some cold case murders that took place after Katrina. It looks as though it involves satanic abuse by members of an occult."

Brigitte clanked the gin bottle against her glass and turned around. "An occult? The paper didn't say anything about Satanism. What proof do you have?"

Cory placed his hand on Marie's knee and stopped her from answering. "There isn't any real proof. It's all speculation right now, but some things are leaning in that direction. You seem a bit shocked by this Brigitte."

Philippe stood up behind Brigitte and finished making her martini. "I don't think it's necessarily shocking as it is disbelief. Everyone always seems to equate New Orleans with voodoo and the occult. There is some history that surrounds those religions, but hardly has there ever been any real substantial proof that it exists. I guess we locals tend to get a little testy when visitors come into town and spew their speculations."

"I don't think we're spewing anything. You asked a question, and Marie answered you. Her visions have been spot-on with everything that has turned up on these murdered women." Gale narrowly eyed Philippe and Brigitte.

"And what visions have you been having, if I may ask?" André stylishly sipped at his scotch.

"I'm not sure if I can reveal any of that to you. It would

probably impede the investigation." Marie looked questionably at Cory.

"She's correct. I don't think it'd be wise if we shared any of the details. It's not that we wouldn't want to; I think we need to keep a tight lid on what we have right now, which hasn't led to any answers. I think we've possibly shared too much as it is regarding the occult."

Brigitte looked at the BEPS team. "Well, we'll promise to keep that information to ourselves, won't we?"

"Oh, of course, we will. We want whoever is doing these murders behind bars as much as anyone. I think it's horrible how the crime has risen since Katrina." Philippe sat down again and pressed his hands to the top of his thighs.

"Well, it's getting a bit late, and I know I've had enough to drink." Marie stood up and looked at André. "Thank you so much for having us in your home and allowing us to watch the reveal. It was an amazing investigation. We especially enjoyed using your equipment. I think we're going to be adding a few things to our inventory."

"We enjoyed having you along. Maybe I'll see you at the next Veterinarian convention. I think they said it's being held in Los Angeles."

"Sure, maybe. I'll have to organize the funds for it. I don't think my little clinic in Sullivan's Island is as busy as yours here in the French Quarter." Marie looked at Gale and motioned her head toward the door. "Again, we thank you all for allowing us in on your meeting and taking part in the investigation from beginning to end. It's been very enlightening."

Jason stood up and shook Marie's hand. "It's been our pleasure. If you're ever back in New Orleans, come on over to the Napoleon House, dinner and drinks are on me."

"We will, the food is amazing; you'd better hang onto your chef."

Gale rushed out after Marie and waited until they were out of earshot and stopped at the curb. "Okay, now that was weird. Why did you rush us out of there so quickly? Especially after the snide comments Brigitte and Philippe were alluding to. It just infuriates me how they still don't seem to believe you're having visions."

Marie smiled and shook her head. "It is refreshing to have you as my best friend. Look, it's okay because I don't care what they believe or don't believe. Everyone looks at the paranormal differently. Take our own Harry, he's very scientific, and hasn't completely accepted my ability."

"Oh, please, don't bring Harry into this conversation."

"Well, it's true. He was a bit skeptical when I started having the visions of the women hung on Sullivan's Island. That's part of the rub between the two of you, am I right?"

Tim replied, "Yes, it is."

Cory pointed at the group of people waiting at the median. "Here's the stop for the trolley."

Marie turned Gale toward her and held onto her shoulders. "But that's okay because I know I'm helping solve these murders. I'm gaining a lot of confidence, and I'm not about to let anyone deter me from that confidence. Besides, that isn't why I wanted to rush out of there."

"I knew there was something else going on. You had that odd look on your face when you motioned for me to leave."

Marie saw the trolley and then looked back at everyone. "Yeah, there was. André's mother was there, and she bugged me through the whole evening to make him aware of it."

Gale's eyes grew wide, and her mouth dropped open. "Shut up, are you serious? What was she doing?"

Cory followed Marie to the trolley. "Is that why you kept squeezing my knee?"

"Yes, let's sit down first, and I'll share with you what Janine

Danél had to say about her son." Marie climbed the trolley steps and slipped her money into the ticket machine.

"Janine... she told you her first name?" Tim slid next to Gale behind Marie and Cory.

"Yep, and she's furious over the fact that André is... let's see, how did she put it... oh, that he is having coitus with Brigitte and it's détruire sa réputation. And from what I can remember from French class, it means Brigitte is ruining his reputation."

Gale slapped Tim's knee. "I knew they were sleeping together. And good ol' Mama Janine is upset. Isn't that something. What else did she say?"

"She rambled on quite a bit, and some of it was very hard to understand, but I think for the most part she wasn't thrilled having Brigitte in her house." Marie chuckled and leaned her back against the window of the trolley. "Oh, and she definitely thought Brigitte drank too much."

"Why didn't you say anything to André in private? I know he would have believed you. He believes in psychics." Cory looked out the window and checked the street signs.

"I did think of telling him, but there wasn't a time when someone else wasn't around."

Tim struggled to keep his leg out of the aisle. "How did Janine know you were able to see her?"

"I'm not very good at averting my eyes. She stood next to André playing hostess while he greeted us at the door. She immediately saw me looking at her and began babbling in my ear. At first, it sounded like a high-pitched humming, but once I focused on her lips, it began to slow down to my frequency level." Marie saw Canal Street and pulled the cord. "Here we are. That wasn't a very long ride."

"Wow, that is so cool. What did she look like?" Gale followed Tim up the aisle.

"She reminded me of Audrey Hepburn, very demure and

proper. She was beautiful."

Cory pulled his cell phone out and checked his messages. "Hey, wait a minute, everyone. I have a text message here from Jesse. It looks like they have some more information and Laura Faye's family will be at the station tomorrow morning for an interview. Marie, he's hoping you can meet him there at nine and watch the interview. He said he'd fill us in on the new evidence."

"It looks as though we're heading to the station tomorrow." Marie looked at Gale and Tim. "Why don't you join us? I think it helps to have your insight too."

"I thought you'd never ask." Gale rubbed her hands together and smiled. "I think we make a pretty good investigative team... paranormal or otherwise."

"Good, then it's settled." Marie grabbed Cory's arm and jogged across the street to the hotel. "Let's meet for breakfast in our room at sevenish. That should give us enough time to eat."

"Sounds like a plan." Gale pressed tight against Tim and shuffled through the revolving door of the hotel.

They reached their floor and said goodnight before entering their rooms. The experience of seeing and hearing Janine Danél exhilarated Marie. Every day brought on newfound skills with her ability and increased her confidence. She only hoped she would be able to be as effective for Jesse at the interview in the morning.

But that was tomorrow, and now she had the love of her life slowly kissing her neck as they headed toward the bed. She loved seeing his face at night before turning in and upon awakening in the morning. She wondered if she would feel lonely when they returned home to their separate residences. And again, that was another thought to be dealt with at another time. For now, she decided to return Cory's kisses and let herself fall into the magic they both did so well together.

THIRTEEN

Mrs. Johnson's eyes were swollen and red from crying continuously through the interview. Her nose looked permanently pink from rubbing the tissue on it, and her hands shook as she wiped the corners of her eyes. Her poorly dyed blonde uncombed hair lay flat against her head. There was a hollow look in her eyes, and Marie's heart ached to listen to her tiny sobs through the two-way mirrored glass.

Mr. Johnson kept his arm firmly around his wife to keep her from falling out of the chair. His short gray hair was thinning at the top, and his left hand balled into a fist. Marie felt he might explode into a tirade and punch his fist into whatever was in his path. Marie could feel the tension drape around his body.

Commander Irons compassionately patted Mrs. Johnson's hand and offered another tissue. "Mr. and Mrs. Johnson, please know we understand you want to take your daughter home and put her to rest. But with this new evidence, we will need to keep her for more tests from the pathologist."

"How can you be sure my baby girl was involved in a cult?" Mrs. Johnson's voice hitched as she dabbed her eyes again.

Jesse quietly replied, "It wasn't a cult. It was the occult. She was involved with Satanism and satanic rituals."

Mr. Johnson shot out of his chair, slamming his fist on the table. "That's the most ridiculous thing I have ever heard. My daughter had an amazing faith in God, and there is no way she was involved in any satanic ritual. I think you have your information wrong, and I think this interview is over. We want to take our daughter home now and get some closure. This is absurd."

Mrs. Johnson grabbed her husband's hand and pulled him back into his chair. "Walter, please sit down. There are some things I need to tell you and Commander Irons that I didn't say before."

Walter sat down and looked absently at his wife. "What do you mean?"

Mrs. Johnson stared at her husband for a few seconds and then directed her attention to Jesse. "When we first received the call of what happened to our baby Laura Faye, I couldn't believe that first, she could have been pregnant, and second, someone would have murdered her for the baby. She had become distant shortly after she moved to New Orleans. Her emails were vague, and she didn't seem to laugh as much as she used to when she would call. Eventually, her phone calls became less and less, and when I would call her, I would always get her voicemail."

"Jenny, you never told me any of this. Why would you keep this from me?"

"Because you were so overprotective of her, I didn't want to push her further away. You know how strained your relationship was with her after she told us she wanted to move out. Walter, she was twenty-three years old and needed her space."

Jenny pulled a black book from her purse and looked at Jesse. "I went up to her room after that call and started looking through her desk. She used to keep a diary, but I couldn't find it. But what I did find was this bible."

Jesse took the black book from her and read the title. "The Satanic Bible, Anton Szandor LaVey. Yes, I've heard about this, but I've never seen one. You say you found this in your daughter's room?"

"Yes, it was taped to the bottom of one of the drawers. I don't know how long it has been there. It frightened me, and I didn't think much about it until you called to tell us how you thought she was murdered." Jenny dropped her face into her hands and shook her head. "I want you to do whatever it takes to find the person or persons responsible for my daughter's horrific death. I want to see them punished. And I want to know why this happened to her. I want to know why she changed and started believing in this garbage."

"Mrs. Johnson, I'm not sure if we'll ever be able to answer those questions for you." Jesse looked up at the glass. "But I have someone here who can shed a little light on this subject if you wish to talk with her. I've been working with a psychic medium that can hold an object of someone's belongings and get a vision from it. Her name is Dr. Marie Bartek, and she is a veterinarian from Sullivan's Island, SC. It was Marie who gave us the insight that your daughter was murdered in a satanic ritual."

"What are you saying? I don't believe any of this." Walter stood up and began to pace behind his wife. "A psychic medium who claims my daughter was murdered in a satanic ritual? We don't believe in psychics, and we certainly don't believe in a satanic bible and rituals." He sat back down and looked at his wife. "Jenny, don't tell me you're going to sit here and listen to this."

"I'll do whatever it takes to understand what happened to our daughter and why she became so engrossed in Satanism. I can't bear the thought of her suffering the way she did and me not being there to help her." Jenny dropped her head into her hands and began to sob.

Walter pulled his wife into his arms and ran his hand over her head. "Okay, yes, I want to know too. Please don't cry anymore. I love you, Jenny."

Jesse slowly stood up. "Why don't I give you two a few minutes to yourselves? I'll bring you more water, and when you are ready, I can bring Dr. Bartek in if you wish to speak with her."

Jenny raised her head, and solemnly looked at Jesse. "Thank you, and yes we would like to speak with her. I want to know my baby's in a better place."

Jesse left the interview room and came through the door where everyone waited. "Marie, I know what you're going to say. I just felt helpless and wanted to give her some relief. I shouldn't have stated you would help her."

Marie turned from the two-way glass and smiled. "It's okay. I don't mind. I'll see what I can do."

"Were you able to pick up anything while you listened to them?"

"Only grief and pain. I will need a few minutes before I go in and speak with them. I need to do a protection prayer. I've never actually done a reading, but I want to help them."

Cory touched Marie's shoulder. "Are you going to be okay in there?"

"Yes, I'll be fine because my spirit guides are right here." Marie kissed Cory's cheek and walked out of the room.

Gale stared at Cory and Tim. "Did she just say here spirit guides were here? Okay, I'm going to need to sit down now."

Jesse sat next to the media technician and watched Marie

enter the room on the monitor. "Make sure you have the recorder on for this. I want to be sure we capture everything."

Marie smiled at Jenny and Walter and sat down across the table. "Hello, my name is Marie Bartek. First, I wanted to give you my sympathy for your loss. Second, what is it you wish to find out about Laura Faye?"

Jenny blew her nose and cleared her throat. "I'm not sure, to be honest with you. I've never really believed in psychics or people being able to see into the future or talk to the dead. Is that what you are able to do?"

Marie weighed her answer carefully and tried to ignore Walter's blank stare. "Well, I have to be honest and tell you I've not actually done a reading for anyone before. I've had this ability since I was a young girl, but never really developed it. It's been the last six or seven months, where I've learned a great deal about myself and my ability. Do you have a small personal object of Laura Faye's that I can hold?"

Jenny absently reached into her purse and pulled out a small gold necklace. "Yes, this was her first holy communion necklace. We gave it to her when she was eight."

Marie took the necklace and smiled at her spirit, guides and closed her eyes. "Yes, I can see Laura Faye in her white dress. She's wearing white gloves and a white satin headband. She's smiling and seems very happy."

Jenny gasped. "Yes, she just loved her dress and gloves. But she argued with me about the headband. She didn't want it messing up her curls."

"I'm seeing her older now. She's dancing in front of a mirror singing into a hairbrush." Marie chuckled at the vision. "Another girl is standing next to her laughing. She has long red hair."

"That's Laura Faye's best friend, Denisa. They used to dance and sing for hours like that."

Marie suddenly felt a cold chill run along her arm, and her head began to ache. The vision changed from happy and carefree to pain and anger. "She's here with us now."

Jenny jumped and grabbed Walter's hand. "Is she okay? What is she doing? Is she saying anything?"

Marie carefully kept her concentration on Laura Faye's lips and remained focused on staying in control. "She's hard to understand. They tend to speak in a different frequency as we do. She's holding her stomach, and I can make out that she's sorry. She's so very sorry for disappointing you."

Jenny spoke out into the empty room. "It's okay Laura baby, Mommy and Daddy aren't disappointed in you. We could never be disappointed in you."

"She's trying to tell me something about the baby. The baby wasn't supposed to die. She wanted to keep the baby, but they wouldn't let her." Marie turned a deaf ear to Jenny and Walter and began a conversation with Laura Faye. "Laura, can you tell me who wouldn't let you keep the baby? You must speak slower so I can understand you. "

Jenny stood frozen in her seat and stared at Marie. "What is she saying?"

Walter waited for a response and shouted at Jenny. "What the hell is going on? How do we know she's telling us the truth?"

Marie heard buzzing in her ears and began to feel nauseated and began swatting her hand at the sudden appearance of flies swarming around her head. "Laura, you're fading in and out. Something is standing in your way and won't allow me to hear you."

Before Marie could focus on Laura Faye's face, she spotted out of the corner of her left eye, slithering on the ceiling, a grotesque creature. She froze and found herself being drawn toward it and couldn't pull her eyes away from its glowing golden eyes. Its skin was covered in scales like a fish and had three tails swishing in different directions. At the end of each tail was a sharp dagger swirling in the air thrashing at Laura Faye, keeping her from coming forward to Marie. Its legs and arms were beast-like with exposed ligaments and muscles. There were sharp claws at the end of its hands and feet.

Marie called out to Laura Faye to move closer to her and the white light. The beast became angrier and reared its horned head toward Laura Faye and threw her back behind it. Marie began to choke and gag but remained strong and willed the beast back with her mind. It squealed and bared its daggered teeth and spat at Marie. Laura Faye began to walk toward Marie, and as fast as the beast appeared, the room became dark, and Marie felt someone slapping her face.

Cory yelled in Marie's ears. "Marie, wake up, please wake up. What's happening? Where are you? Are you okay?"

Marie slowly opened her eyes and began to thrash in Cory's arms. "I've got to save her from it. It has her in its powers and won't let her go."

Jesse helped Cory hold Marie still. "Marie, you're okay, you're with us here in the police station. You're okay."

Marie finally saw Cory's face come into focus and gradually saw Jenny and Walter Johnson huddled in the corner, holding onto each other sobbing. "I'm okay, what happened? Why is the chair on the floor and the mirror broken?"

Cory helped Marie up into the chair and cupped her face in his hands. "Are you seeing me clearly now? Marie is that you?"

"Of course it's me, why are you asking me that? What happened?" Marie leaned over and felt as if she would vomit. "Oh, wow, it's beginning to come back to me. I couldn't hear Laura Faye clearly enough because something was standing in her way, and then all of a sudden, there were flies everywhere.

They kept flying in my mouth, and my eyes and I couldn't see her anymore. Then up on the ceiling was this horrible beast. It had horns and claws and daggers for teeth and three tails. It had these horrific golden eyes, and it wouldn't let Laura Faye near me. It spat at me."

Jesse hurriedly moved the Johnson's out of the room. "Mr. and Mrs. Johnson I'm so sorry for what you witnessed. I had no idea this was going to happen. Please accept my humblest apologies."

Marie looked at Cory. "What the hell happened? What did they see? What did you see?"

Gale slowly walked over to Marie and lightly touched her hand. "Marie, you were possessed. It was the scariest thing I've ever seen. You were talking in tongue and spatting at the Johnson's. You had this massive strength and threw the chair at the two-way glass and shattered it. It all happened so fast. We couldn't get in the room. The door handle wouldn't budge. I thought Cory and Jesse were going to have heart attacks."

"I think I did." Tim sat next to Marie and rubbed her shoulder. "Are you sure you're okay, Marie? You scared the hell out of us."

"I lost complete control. I was beginning to understand what she was telling me when that thing showed up. It's strange though, I wasn't afraid of it. Even with it flailing Laura Faye back behind it and spitting at me, I held my ground. I kind of remember it stating its name."

Cory, Gale, and Tim said in unison. "Beelzebub."

"That's right." Marie looked at the three of them and began to rub her temples. "What else did it say?"

"Well, I'm sure Jesse could run the tape back for you. They recorded everything." Gale poured Marie a glass of water and handed it to her.

"Yeah, I need to see it, because from the look that the three of you are giving me, I'm beginning to wonder if I have three tails."

Marie sat in horror, watching herself speak in a voice she knew wasn't her own. She was laughing a hideous laugh and speaking a language she never heard before. The Johnson's screamed and cried in the corner as Marie hissed at them in a foreign language. At the exact moment, Marie remembered willing Laura Faye into the light was when she picked up the chair and threw it into the two-way glass. It was then that Marie briefly remembered her spirit guides casting the beast away and witnessed herself pass out on the floor.

"I don't feel so well." Marie took another gulp of water.

"What the hell just happened in there? How am I going to explain any of this to my superiors?" Jesse shut off the video and looked at Cory.

"You're going to show them this recording. It's obvious Marie was possessed by Beelzebub." Cory continued to rub Marie's back.

"First, we have to remember not to state its name. You only give it more power that way. The Johnson's must think I'm a complete whack job."

Gale shook her head. "They don't think you're a whack job. None of us do, you pretty much scared the hell out of everyone, but I think it's pretty obvious there was a darker force in there that didn't want you communicating with Laura Faye. Can you remember anything else that happened or was said?"

"No, I couldn't get everything Laura Faye was trying to tell me." Marie looked at Jesse. "I'm sorry. I told you I was still getting a hold on all of this. You did volunteer me."

Jesse nodded. "It's okay. It wasn't your fault. I'm just glad you're okay. You really freaked me out. Do you have any idea what language that was?"

"I'm guessing Latin." Tim shrugged at everyone staring back at him. "Sorry, I studied it in college."

Gale asked, "Could you make any of that out?"

"It's been a while, but I was thinking of asking for a copy of this to take back and play for the SIPS team. Maybe between Harry and me, we may be able to decipher what was being said."

"That's an excellent idea." Marie stood up and addressed Jesse. "Can we have a copy of the video?"

"Sure, we're going to need help on figuring it all out too. I'll get Skip to burn a copy for you." Jesse paused at the door. "Marie, even though you freaked the Johnson's out, they did believe you were telling them the truth about seeing Laura Faye. They also believe there was something very evil that led to her death. They wanted me to thank you."

Marie smiled, "Thanks for telling me that. I need all of the support I can get. Hey, before I forget, you told Cory yesterday that you had more evidence."

"Oh, that's right, we got some other cellular traces from the burned baby, and we're running it through the database to see if there are any matches. If we're lucky, we'll be able to find out who the father is, and who may have played a part in her death. Hopefully, it'll lead us to this occult."

Cory grabbed Marie's hands and firmly held them. "I think once we get the copy of this video, you need to get some rest back at the hotel. We can call the team after you've rested. You're looking pretty pale right now."

"I hope I can rest. I can't get the picture of that beast out of my head."

"I can help do some research when we get back. I'll see what I can find on this... shall we call him Demon B?" Gale smiled and patted Marie's forearm.

"It's better than stating his full name and thanks for helping out. Thanks to all of you for sticking by my side. I'm surprised you haven't run off after witnessing all of that."

"Well, quite frankly, we're all too scared to after seeing you whip that chair around." Tim smiled wide.

Gale chuckled and elbowed Tim in the side. "Let's get out of here. I still feel as if something is watching us."

"Speaking of watching, before you went into the interview room, you mentioned your spirit guides were here. Are they still here?" Cory helped Marie out of the chair.

"Yes, they are. In fact, it was they who willed that beast out of the room. I had this incredible amount of strength at the last minute when I was trying to help Laura Faye into the light. When that beast, for lack of a better phrase, reared its ugly head, they made it disappear. They protected me, yet again."

"Good, I'm glad," Cory spoke absently into the room. "Thank you for watching over her."

They retrieved the copy of the video and agreed to meet up with the SIPS team after lunch and have a long chat. It was time they started to pull everyone's knowledge base into this investigation to better understand it all.

The whole encounter completely drained Marie, but somehow renewed her as well. Being possessed wasn't up on her list of things to experience, but she felt satisfied that she stood firm. She planned on seeing this case through to the end, no matter how hard the dark side tried to stop her.

FOURTEEN

Marie tossed and turned in her sleep and continued to replay the vision in her head. She was able to pick up pieces of the conversation she had with Laura Faye, but it didn't make any sense. She awoke abruptly to the sound of muffled voices in the outer room and decided to get up and join them.

Marie smiled at everyone and grabbed a bottle of water. "I must say, I'm beginning to get used to seeing all of you every time I wake up."

"You don't look any more rested. Did you sleep at all?" Cory walked over to Marie and softly kissed her lips.

"No, not really, I couldn't get that beast out of my head. But I did remember a few more things that Laura Faye was trying to tell me."

"We've been doing quite a bit of research and found some information on that beast. Why don't you grab some coffee and join us? We can share everything with the SIPS team. I'm supposed to Skype them as soon as you got up. They're all waiting at headquarters." Gale pulled the laptop open and began to log in to her account.

"Sounds good, I may have to have one of these beignets. I'm also going to need a pad and pen to write down what I remembered before I forget again." Marie stuffed the powdered dough into her mouth and poured a cup of coffee.

Gale's computer chimed, and she answered the beep. "Hey, everyone, how's it going? Marie's up and ready to fill you in on her vision. Have you come up with any information?"

Myra wore a look of concern. "Hello, Marie, I have been worried sick about you. How are you, and how have you recovered from this possession?"

Marie took a sip of coffee and smiled at her mentor. "I'm okay, a little disjointed, but I think my crystals have protected me, along with my spirit guides."

"Good, I'm glad you've been keeping them close. Now dear, why don't you fill us in on exactly what happened at the police station? Gale, Tim, and Cory told us their side of what they witnessed. I'm afraid this time I wasn't aware of anything happening. I normally pick up on when you're in danger. I have a feeling this demon blocked my path." Myra's bracelets jingled in the background.

"Well, first I want to tell you what bits and pieces I remembered from Laura Faye before we were rudely interrupted by this demon. She wanted me to convey to her parents that she was sorry for disappointing them. Then she said she wanted to keep the baby and didn't want it to die. It sounds to me she must have changed her mind or didn't know they were going to sacrifice the baby."

Harry appeared on the monitor. "It would make sense that they led her to believe the baby would be used in some other way, and she didn't know they were going to sacrifice it."

"Right, then when Demon B appeared and tried to keep her from entering the light, Laura Faye mouthed some things that I remember, but it doesn't make sense to me. The sentences were a bit broken up, but she said something about high in the hierarchy. Then I think she said people aren't as they seem and not to trust them." Marie took another bite of her beignet.

Gale grabbed Tim's laptop and placed it next to hers. "Okay, well, we've been reading up on this Demon B character and found a little bit about him. Marie, you stated that you saw flies all over the place right before the beast emerged. It appears he was known as Lord of the Flies. He was placed high in Hell's hierarchy. So that makes sense what you heard from Laura Faye. He led a revolt against Satan and was placed among the three most prominent fallen angels."

Harry interrupted Gale. "This is true, and he was associated with the deadly sins of pride and gluttony."

Gale smiled, "Right and he was frequently named as a supplication by confessed witches. Down through history, he has been held responsible for many cases of demon possession, and his name came up frequently during the Salem witch trials."

"Wow, well, it seems to sort of fit with everything."

Mimi turned their laptop toward her. "Tim, why don't you and Harry play back the video and decipher the Latin Marie... or should I say Demon B, was saying."

Tim pulled his laptop closer to the Skype screen. "Okay, here's one of the parts the demon said through her. The phrase was, Quomodo audebas me ad vos, which means, how dare you come against me?"

Harry spoke up and moved closer to Mimi's monitor. "And then there's the laughter, which shows Marie laughing, but I get the feeling he was laughing at Marie. And the next thing it says is, Nunquam enim eam esse ad infernum damnatorum, which means, you will never have her, she has been damned to Hell."

Gale squirmed in her chair as she watched the video again. "Yeah, I'm beginning to have a terrible feeling about all of this. I'm assuming he was talking about Laura Faye?"

"Yes, he was, no matter how hard I or my spirit guides tried, we couldn't get her to cross into the light." Marie sighed and leaned back in her chair.

Harry leaned closer to the screen. "Marie, the description you gave of Demon B is accurate. He was worshipped in the Philistine city of Ekron. In later Christian and Biblical sources, he appeared as a demon and the name of one of the seven princes of Hell."

"Gee he sounds more and more intriguing... not. What I don't understand is why did this thing show up in Marie's vision? I don't understand the connection." Gale stopped the video and began to open a bottle of wine.

"It's very possible the occult was making their sacrifice to this demon. There is a correlation between good and evil, as you know so it wouldn't be unusual for this group to be worshiping Beelz... I mean, Demon B." Harry shifted his glasses up his nose.

"What makes people do this kind of thing? How can they join such an evil group and do such evil things?" Gale gulped down her glass of Merlot.

"Many psychiatrists have found that people want to belong. And sometimes, wanting to belong desperately enough brings them to do anything. Intense situations create strong solidarity." Harry shifted and looked at Cory. "What were the forensic results regarding any drugs found in this Laura Faye's system?"

"They need to run some more detailed tests. Jesse hadn't given us any of that information." Cory sipped Marie's coffee. "But they did find some new DNA from the baby remains, and they're going to see if it matches who fathered the child."

"That would be a great piece of evidence. I would imagine

if they didn't find drugs in Laura Faye's system originally when they run these detailed tests, they would find either imovane or its generic name zopiclone. These drugs are powerful, and it is possible Laura Faye had no idea she was being drugged or what they planned for her baby." Harry wiped his brow with his familiar crumpled handkerchief.

Cory sat up in his chair. "Marie, didn't you say Laura Faye was very friendly with the stranger in the vision you had of them in the pub right before she was murdered?"

"Yes, she was, and I believe she was drugged then because I could feel how listless and dizzy she was."

Tim continued to listen carefully to the video. "Hey, Harry, did you listen to the last part of this video before Marie passed out? I need a little help with deciphering the words."

"Actually, I hadn't got to that part yet. Let me play our video on our end for a minute and see what I can come up with."

Gale looked at Tim and leaned in closer to hear the video. "Can you possibly run it in slow motion to pick it up any easier and wear the earphones?"

"Yeah, I could try that." Tim plugged in the earphones and began to replay the last few minutes of the video.

"Myra, while they're busy figuring that out, how is it possible for it to have blocked your path?" Marie shifted in her seat and sipped more coffee.

"I believe while this demon had possession of you, it obstructed anyone who had telepathic communication with you using a sort of psychic static."

"And that means exactly how it sounds, right?"

"Yes, it's a form of a psychic blocking defense. Marie, this isn't anything like you've dealt with. It's nothing I've ever dealt with. This is pure evil and has powers you can't even begin to understand. I think you're going to need to stay in touch with

Harry as much as possible. I've also sent a package to you. It should arrive there tomorrow and contains a red jade stone which is a powerful stone used for divination practice, worn to protect you during out of body experiences and vision quests by providing a solid grounding. I've also included a blood stone."

Marie replied, "Blood stone, I've heard of that before."

"I'm sure you have dear. It is a warrior stone for overcoming obstacles, calming one's fear of a real or perceived enemy, and it helps in maintaining blood harmony. I have fit both of these stones into a ring and have placed a protection prayer over them. I want you to wear this ring at all times, Marie. Do not, at any time, take it off." Myra faintly smiled at Marie.

Marie smiled back, feeling the warmth squeeze her heart. "Thank you, Myra. What would I do without you?"

Harry cleared his throat and moved in view on the monitor. "Marie, I think you'd better listen carefully. I just rewound that last portion of the video and translated Latin into English."

"Well, don't just sit there, Harry, what did it say?" Gale shook her head and sighed.

Harry wiped his brow. "It said, Lorem ipsum dolor vobis commisso omnium Marie cito, which means, I look forward to you joining us all, Marie... very soon."

Gale shot out of her chair and began to pace around the room. "Okay, well, that's enough, that's all I needed to hear. I think we need to step away from this whole case. This isn't funny anymore. This Demon B has just made it personal for you, Marie. I don't like it."

"I think I agree with Gale. Marie, Jesse would understand if you didn't want to continue to help him. I don't like this either. Plus, you haven't sat through an interview with the first victim's family yet." Cory leaned forward and held Marie's hands.

Mimi forced her way to the front of the group and leaned in toward the camera. "Marie, I think we all agree on this one. I think it's best to let the rest of the investigation to the police. If this Jesse is as good as Cory has stated he is... then let him do his job."

Marie turned away from Cory and looked into the laptop. "I appreciate all of your concerns, truly I do. But I just can't stop helping. Besides, I don't think Laura Faye is going to let me. She's not the only victim. Jesse feels strong about this being the same occult that killed the women from his cold case. Maybe sitting with the other victim's parents, I'll get more evidence to help." She turned back toward Cory and smiled. "You know I can't turn my back on this, please don't ask me to."

Cory dropped his head into Marie's hands and kissed the tips of her fingers. "I know, okay, but I stay close to you every second. We all do. And we've already got a detective following us for protection, but I don't want any of us separating. Those are strict orders."

"You got it, Chief." Tim saluted and smiled.

Myra leaned forward and replied, "Marie, we are all going to continue to research as much as we can on this, and I'm going now to begin meditating and placing a protection prayer around all of you. I think you should do the same."

"I will Myra, already had that as first on my agenda." Marie smiled at the wonderful group of friends staring back at her. "Thank you again, all of you, for your wonderful support. We really do make a great team, don't we?"

Marie logged off the computer and retreated to her room. She closed the door and lit the candles she got from Delia and pulled out the crystal necklace from beneath her shirt. Her spirit guides were waiting for her as she sat on the bed in a yoga position and closed her eyes. Through her thoughts, she visualized the white light of protection around her and began to meditate. Feeling the positive power and energy surround her, she smiled and stated her intentions.

HE SLAPPED the beady-eyed man and knocked him to the floor. "You fool. Because you didn't get rid of the baby's remains, we now have evidence left behind. They can now trace it back to its mother and possibly me."

The pathetic little man stayed on the ground and kept his arms over his face. "We did the best we could master. There was no way the baby could be found. We made sure of it."

"Apparently, you didn't because they did find the baby." He looked at the two assistants and gestured his hand in a dismissing fashion. "Take care of him and be sure it's made to look like an accident. I'm tired of dealing with incompetence."

She listened to the wretched cries echo behind her and turned toward him. "So why did you call me here tonight? I thought you had tired of me."

"I need you to be sure that the police haven't moved any further on their investigation. I don't care how just take care of it. We need to stop this from spiraling out of control." He shrugged off her outstretched hand on his arm. "We also need to move the bodies and dispose of them. I think you can handle that, no?"

"And what if I refuse?"

He slowly turned toward her and cocked his head to the left. "Then you'll discover what true pain and sacrifice really is. You're in this as deep as I am, if not deeper. Don't decide to become righteous. It doesn't suit you."

She stared at him through narrowed eyes. "Very well, I'll see to it that the bodies are disposed of properly. Perhaps if you had let me do it originally, we wouldn't be standing here trying to cover our tracks. Didn't I tell you there are always trails left behind?"

"So you did, so let's see how loyal and creative you are in carrying out my request. I want nothing left behind." He whipped around and left her standing alone.

FIFTEEN

JESSE IRONS TOOK a break from reading the ME report and motioned for Cory and Marie to sit down in his office. "I'm glad you were both able to come back down to the station. Marie, how are you feeling?"

"I'm okay now. We had a group meeting with the SIPS team. I was able to get some information on the demon that possessed me. I was also able to do some more meditating to help clear my mind."

"That's great. Well, first, I wanted to let you both know that we weren't able to get any conclusive evidence on the other DNA traces that were found on the baby remains."

"I thought you said you did." Marie furrowed her brow.

"We did, but the DNA was contaminated." Jesse held up his hand and continued. "Getting results from burnt remains is difficult enough, but known DNA samples from the perpetrator and victim would have to be obtained and tested to determine whether they could be contributors to the mixed DNA profile."

Cory surmised, "So basically because you had Laura Faye's

body, you were able to obtain a DNA sample from her to match to the baby remains. Only having the other trace of DNA and nobody to match it up with, the results are too difficult to give a conclusive result."

Jesse sighed and leaned back in his chair. "Exactly, I knew it was a long shot, but it was worth going the extra mile to see if it would result in finding who fathered the child."

"So we're no further than we were. We still don't know who impregnated Laura Faye." Marie stood up and began to pace in the small office space.

"Well, yes, and no. The other forensic report does show drugs in Laura Faye's system. After detailed testing, they found traces of zopiclone, which is a generic hypnotic drug. So we can conclusively say she was drugged, and this is a known process in satanic rituals."

"That's something I guess. What about the other parents of the first victim, what were their names? When will they be here for an interview? I want to sit down with them as well, and see if I can come up with anything." Marie felt better, knowing she could still offer some help.

"The first victim was Anna Beth Montgomery, and Mr. and Mrs. Montgomery will be here this afternoon for an interview." Jesse hesitated and then continued. "But you aren't allowed to be a part of the interview."

Marie turned on her heels and stared down at Jesse. "Why not? I was able to learn quite a bit of information for the Johnson's and this investigation."

"I know, and I'm grateful. But I told you it was going to be hard to explain all of this to my superiors. They saw the video and flat out refused for you to be involved in the case. They don't believe in psychics, even though they couldn't explain why your voice dropped quite a few octaves and didn't sound natural. They also couldn't explain why you were speaking in Latin."

"This is absurd. Couldn't you convince them of my ability? I'm not some causal psychic medium doing this for attention. These women came to me in a plea for help to find their killers. As I told the SIPS team and Cory earlier, I can't stop now." Marie slumped into a chair and dropped her face into her hands.

"Marie, please know that I do believe in your ability. You've given us leads that we wouldn't have had otherwise, and I explained that to my superiors. But these men are also men who find answers based on facts and science." Jesse walked over to Marie and placed his hand on her shoulder. "I don't plan on keeping you out of the loop. I'm willing to take the risk of being put on suspension. I still need you to help with this case. This has haunted me for far too long. We need to put an end to this heinous crime spree and lock these psychos up for life, or better yet, put them on death row."

Marie slowly slid her hands off her face and looked up at Jesse. "Thank you. I appreciate your faith in me. Cory was right... you are open-minded and good at what you do."

Jesse smiled and glanced at Cory. "I'm going to need you both to retrace the areas where we found Anna Beth and Laura Faye. If Marie can pick up on things the way she has, then there may be a possibility of her having a connection or a vision where the bodies were found."

"That sounds like the logical next step." Cory tightly held Marie's hand.

"Yes, I think that's a great idea." Marie sat up straight with renewed hope. "Do you think you would be able to sneak something out of Anna Beth's? I know it may be risky, but if I could handle something of hers, I may be able to get more details."

"I think I may be able to persuade a few forensic pals of

mine to cooperate. I may need a little more time on that, though." Jesse walked back behind his desk and sat down. "In the meantime, you will continue to have protection. I had my superiors concede on that one. And as always, stick together and watch your backs and contact me as soon as you have any new leads."

"So we're standing at the end of Canal Street doing what again?" Gale stood with her hands on her hips. "I'm a little ticked Jesse's so-called superiors don't want you working on the case."

"Jesse wanted me to go back to where they found the bodies to see if I'm able to come up with any new evidence, and I can't blame them for not wanting me involved, I'm a civilian and a liability. In their minds, they have enough victims, plus they don't believe in psychics." Marie breathed in deeply and closed her eyes. "Cory, how far away is that Beachcorner bar and grill?"

"It's only about two blocks from here."

"I think I may want to go there next. I'm not getting anything at the spot where they found Laura Faye. I think this is where they dumped her. It feels as if they were in a hurry."

"I wouldn't mind getting a burger." Tim shrugged at everyone staring at him. "I didn't eat much of a lunch."

"I suppose I could stomach a burger and a beer." Cory slapped Tim on the back.

"Yeah, I could drink... maybe it'll cool my temper." Gale smiled and cocked her right eyebrow.

"Good because I keep feeling this pull to go there." Marie slipped her hand into Cory's and cuddled against him.

Cory asked, "What kind of a pull?"

"Well, I think this is the pub I saw Laura Faye in the earlier vision. The one right before she was murdered."

"Oh, great, now I really want a drink." Gale jogged across the street to keep up with Tim.

Tim stopped in front of the bar and looked at the neon-lit name. "Hey, cool palm tree."

Marie chuckled and walked through the door. "Wow, it's dark in here. I need to let my eyes adjust."

The walls were covered with flat-screen televisions and memorabilia of the Saints football team. Tinsel draped the leather-covered booths lined along the wall at the right just a short distance from the bar on the opposite side of the room. There were people shooting pool off to the back while others mindlessly played slot machines.

"Whoa, check it out, happy hour is from eleven to seven. I think we timed this place perfect." Gale pulled up a bar stool and sat down. "Marie, do you think Jesse will be able to get something for you to hold from that Montgomery girl without anyone finding out?"

"I don't know. I hope so. It could help me out with piecing all of these visions together."

Tim sat next to Gale and grabbed a menu. "Hey, that looks like Brigitte sitting over there in the corner."

"What... where? Oh yeah, it is her. Who's she with, and what's she doing here?" Gale placed her purse on the back of the stool.

Marie rolled her eyes. "It is a free country Gale. She's allowed to eat here. And as far as who she is with, I have no idea."

"Well, it's not André. I figured her for a two-timer." Gale waved the bartender over.

"Let's not start judging her, besides, she doesn't know that we know she's sleeping with André. That information came from Janine, remember?" Marie pulled a stool out to sit down and saw a flash of light and lost her balance.

Cory grabbed Marie's arm. "You okay, what happened?"

"This is definitely the bar Laura Faye was in the night she was murdered. I'd see the same vision over again, only just certain snippets of it."

The bartender walked over to Marie and stared a hole through her. His slicked back carbon hair matched his eyes. He placed a bar napkin in front of Marie. "What can I get you?"

Marie tried to remain calm, but her throat was dry when she spoke. "I'll take a Michelob Amber Bock."

Cory waited for the bartender to walk away. "What's going on? Are you getting a read on him?"

"Yeah, I am." Marie touched the napkin and felt the same shock shoot through her arm. "He was here the night Laura Faye was murdered. He was working and knew what's going on. The cops questioned him, but he lied to them. He said he didn't recognize her."

Cory remained at Marie's side. "What else are you seeing?"

Marie answered in a trancelike state. "He sees Laura Faye and the stranger hanging onto each other. Wait a minute. He slipped something into her glass. He drugged her."

The bartender slammed the beer down on the napkin. "Are you all ordering something off the menu?"

Marie jerked back to the present. "What?"

Cory answered, "Yes, and you can put it all on one bill."

Gale watched the bartender walk away in a huff. "What else did you see?"

"That was it. He slipped something into her drink. That's how she was drugged. He has to be involved in her murder. He looks like he could belong to a satanic group."

"Yeah, but how are the police going to prove any of that if

they don't believe in your ability?" Gale took a sip of Marie's beer. "Is he coming back to take our orders?"

Tim looked up from the menu. "Here comes the bartender and Brigitte."

"What brings you all here today?" Brigitte sat next to Tim and smiled.

Gale answered quickly and nodded her head toward the end of the bar. "Apparently, not the same thing you're here for."

Brigitte looked back toward her seat. "Well, I don't know about y' all, but I'm having lunch... and that's my boss. I work here."

"Oh, that's right, you're a bartender. How long have you worked here?" Cory slipped into detective mode.

"Only about seven months, but I was a bartender in Mississippi for about five years. There's nothin' better than a good bar. Love the atmosphere."

"I can relate to that." Tim smiled.

"You really can't relate to anything right now." Gale squeezed Tim's leg and looked at Brigitte. "We decided to have lunch, heard the burgers were delicious here."

Brigitte stared at Marie. "Yeah, they are, Marie, are you okay? You look a bit pale."

"Yeah, I'm fine. I need to get something to eat." Marie brushed the bartender's arm while handing him the menu and instantly felt nauseated.

The room spun and there standing in front of Marie was a young boy of about ten cowering in the corner of a room covering his face. He screamed and cried as the belt strap slapped across his back and face. The older man holding the belt laughed and yelled at the same time.

Then the room changed, and the same young boy held a match and placed it against the hamster he held in his other hand. The hamster squirmed and squealed as the boy wickedly smiled and choked the life out of it.

Suddenly the same young boy, now about fifteen, carefully carved a pentagram into his forearm. He relished in pain and giggled at the blood dripping down from his arm onto the floor. His eyes were glazed over, and Marie could feel his hate and anger.

The room spun yet again, and Marie found herself standing in a wooded area, watching a satanic ritual. She realized the young boy was the bartender, now about twenty, being initiated into the occult. The room continued to spin, and Marie could only make out bits and pieces of chanting and the smell of incense burning. Trying to control her aching head, Marie peered through the hooded crowd and saw the bartender sexually assaulting a young woman tied to a marble altar as blood spurt everywhere. Marie gasped and grabbed her chest, and the scene disappeared and faded to darkness.

Marie slowly opened her eyes and saw everyone hovering over her. "I can't believe what I just saw."

"Are you okay, Marie, you were all balled up in the fetal position, writhing and screaming." Cory held Marie tightly in his arms. "What on earth did you see?"

Marie spotted the bartender lurking behind the group of people around her. "It was him, the bartender."

"What was him?" Brigitte looked behind her and saw the bartender take off through the kitchen. "You mean Dwayne? You saw a vision about Dwayne?"

"Obviously, that's who she meant, and he just took off through the kitchen." Gale looked back at Marie. "What did you see Marie, because whatever it was, it has him running scared. Don't you think someone should call Jesse?"

"Already on it." Cory held his cell phone and dialed Jesse's number.

SIXTEEN

JESSE FINISHED his conversation with one of the police officers and walked over to where Marie was sitting. "Okay, I got some preliminary information from the group, but I'd like to get the specifics of your vision if you think you can give it to me in detail."

Marie explained her vision and continued to rub her temples. "It's pretty apparent he has what it takes to be involved in these murders."

"Can you give me any more information on what you saw regarding what he slipped into Laura Faye's drink?" Jesse continued to write on his notepad.

"No, only that he dropped a powder into her drink. But I don't know how to prove it. Is anyone going to take my word for it?"

"I don't care if anyone else does, I do. I have a couple of men tracking this Dwayne down." Jesse looked at Brigitte. "How long have you known Dwayne, and what's his last name?"

"He was working here when I started, and I think his last

name is Lucas." Brigitte motioned for her boss to join the conversation. "Larry, how long has Dwayne worked here?"

Larry Peters sauntered over to the group wearing a stained apron tied around his narrow waist. His silver hair was thinning, and his puny arms hung out beneath his rolled-up sleeves. "He's been working here for about a year. Can anyone tell me what's going on?"

Jesse stopped writing. "We'd like to get an address on Dwayne Lucas and bring him into the station for some questioning."

"Questioning about what? This is a hell of a way to approach someone if he fouled up a drink order." Larry leaned against the back of a booth.

"This is a little more involved than fouling up a drink order. Now, can I have an address?"

"Sure, let me go to the back and pull out my files. I'm sure I've got it somewhere." Larry walked back through the kitchen.

Brigitte turned toward Jesse and Cory. "Don't you think it's a little much to go after someone on a vision? I mean, come on, I've been working with him for quite a while, and I never noticed anything unusual." Brigitte looked down at Marie. "Just what exactly was your vision?"

Cory put up his hand. "That's privileged information. We can't divulge anything to you. But have you noticed any markings on his arms, such as a tattoo?"

"No, I haven't paid any attention to his arms. I mean, Dwayne is a little odd and maybe a bit backward, but he's never caused any problems for me or any customers."

Jesse got a call on his radio, and he responded. "Copy that central. We're on our way. It looks like they found Dwayne on Dauphine Street. They came up with some interesting information through NCIC. They're bringing him to the house, but

I'm not going to be able to allow you to go. I still need you to keep a distance from my superiors for now."

Marie stood up. "I understand, just make sure you keep us in the loop on what you find out on this Dwayne, please."

"I will, oh and before I forget, I have a scarf from the Montgomery girl. Maybe we can meet at the Bistro again. I'll be able to fill you in on what we find out on Dwayne Lucas if anything, and I'll bring the scarf with me. I have a feeling we're going to need more proof to wrap up this case."

"I have more than a feeling." Marie waved goodbye to Jesse and looked back at Cory and Gale. "I'm glad I was wearing my ring from Myra. This is going to sound strange, but I was getting that same odd feeling when I got the visit from Bee... I mean, Demon B."

"Did he show up?" Gale sat back down at the bar.

"No, he wasn't around, but this Dwayne Lucas was involved in Laura Faye's murder." Marie pulled the bar stool in and sipped her beer slowly. "He sure did have a messed-up childhood though. I'm not sure who was beating on him in my vision, but it was horrible. No wonder he's all screwed up."

Tim picked up the menu again. "Well, everyone has a choice in life. You can decide to turn your past around and make something of yourself. Or you can blame your past and use it as an excuse."

Cory nodded. "Very well said."

"How in the world are they going to prove that he drugged Laura Faye? There's got to be some other clue or something I missed that can tie him in with this whole thing." Marie continued to rub her temples.

Brigitte came out from the kitchen holding four platters of burgers and fries. "Here, this is on the house. It looks as though I'm on duty now that Dwayne took off."

Tim smiled. "That was nice of you."

Gale rolled her eyes. "Well, I think it's the least you can do after questioning Marie's vision."

"Look, I don't question Marie's vision. I find it pretty hard to believe, I guess." Brigitte looked at Marie. "I mean, I know people have that ability, and I don't doubt that ya do, but to have seen all of that from brushing his arm, it's just way out there for me, ya know?"

"You weren't supposed to know what her vision was." Gale bit into her burger.

"Well, I heard bits and pieces of it."

Marie nibbled on a fry. "I get you have some doubt, and it's way out there for me as well. Look, I don't expect everyone to believe me, really, I don't. But you have to know that I'm not having a blast seeing all of this stuff either. It's very complicated and involved. But I also feel the need to help these women. I believe that's why I've got this gift."

"I guess I didn't think about what it's like for ya to be able to see spirits and have these visions." Brigitte snuck a fry from Gale's plate and ignored her stare. "I have to admit. It's pretty hard to write off what ya saw on our investigation at the LaLaurie House."

Gale snickered. "That's not all she saw."

Brigitte poured a beer for another customer. "What do ya mean?"

Marie elbowed Gale. "Nothing, she didn't mean anything."

"She meant somethin'."

Gale nudged Marie. "Go ahead, tell her. Maybe then she'll believe you have this ability."

"Look, it's really none of our business."

"No, go ahead, I can take it. Is there something else ya saw?" Brigitte wiped the bar down with a bar towel.

"As a matter of fact, I did. It was at André's house." Marie waited for Brigitte to return from waiting on another customer and continued. "When we arrived at André's house, we were greeted at the door by his mother, Janine."

Brigitte's brows went straight up. "You did? How did ya know her name was Janine?"

"Because she told me it was Janine. She also had quite a bit of other things to share with me. She is a bit upset with you."

Brigitte began to stutter. "About me? Why on earth would she be upset about me?"

Gale jumped in to answer. "Because she knows you're sleeping with André, and she's pissed about it."

"Gale, please, I could have told her a little better than that. She's not pissed." Marie shrugged her shoulders.

"Oh yes, she is, she's pissed that they're having coitus." Gale laughed and almost choked on her beer.

Brigitte almost dropped a beer glass. "She told ya that?"

"Well, is it true?" Gale licked the ketchup off her finger.

Brigitte poured another beer from the tap and walked it over to a woman at the end of the bar and walked back and stood in front of Marie. "Okay, yes, it's true. We've been seeing each other for the last four months. It kind of just happened. We weren't tellin' anyone about it."

Tim asked, "Why, what's the big deal?"

"It's not a big deal. It developed on one of our investigations." Brigitte stared at Marie. "Why was Janine so upset?"

"I guess she feels you're ruining his reputation. At least that's what I was able to make out; she was speaking in French." Marie took another bite of her burger.

"Wow, ya know, André has been the one keeping it under wraps. It didn't matter to me if anyone knew. Maybe he's getting a sense from his mother."

"It's possible he is. He's pretty open to the psychic world. His mother and Delia were pretty close."

"Okay, well, I suppose I'm a little more convinced about what you're able to do." Brigitte poured another beer.

"A little more, gee is that all? Look there's a lot more Marie can see regarding this whole case. She saw today that this Dwayne drugged the latest victim right in this bar the night she was brutally murdered." Gale curled up her lip.

"Gale, I think you've said about enough." Cory patted Gale's shoulder. "You need to disregard what you just heard. We can't have any of that getting out, do you understand?"

"Yeah, sure, but Dwayne? I wouldn't have thought that. Why on earth would he drug her?" Brigitte leaned over the bar.

"He belongs to a sick satanic group who enjoy murdering women in sick ways." Gale saw Marie's angered face and stopped talking.

"Gale, you do need to learn to keep things to yourself." Marie looked at Brigitte. "Look, we do need to get going, can you please keep this information to yourself? We're having enough trouble getting proof. We can't afford any of this to get out and ruin any chances the police may have of solving this case."

"No, no, I understand. Just as we said the other night, we want these creeps caught just as much as y' all do." Brigitte began clearing their plates. "I'd also like y' all to keep my secret as well. At least until I find out what's holding André back from telling anyone."

"Sure, of course. Gale shouldn't have said anything, yet again." Marie ignored Gale's questioning look. "It just may be that Janine is from another era and old fashioned. She doesn't believe in coitus before marriage."

"Marriage, well that's certainly not in the plans. I guess she'll have to get over it." Brigitte waved goodbye and continued to wipe down the bar.

Marie followed Gale out the door and shaded her eyes. "Gale, you do need to learn to keep a lid on my visions."

"I know, I know, I'm sorry. I couldn't help it. She's just so smug and talks down to you about what you're able to do. It ticked me off, okay?" Gale looped her hand in Marie's arm. "You're not mad at me, are you? Come on, pal. You're my best friend. Best friends don't get mad."

Marie shook her head. "No, I'm not mad, but you do need to keep my visions about the case to yourself. We don't want to blow any of this."

"I hear ya." Gale turned an imaginary key over her lips. "My lips are sealed from now on."

"That should be interesting." Tim dodged Gale's punch to his arm.

"Why don't we head over toward the convention center. That's where they found the Montgomery girl. I hope I can get a better feel for her. She was who I saw in my first vision." Marie grabbed Cory's hand as they all walked toward the trolley stop.

"WHAT DO you mean they have Lucas in custody? How in the world did they connect him to anything?" He balled his hands into fists. "You were supposed to keep this from happening."

She casually walked over to the window and looked out over Jackson Square. "I wasn't in charge of Dwayne. He's careless and lacks loyalty."

"He was one of my most loyal... don't slander his name in front of me."

"Oh, that's right, he was one of your favorites." She began to snicker.

He grabbed her arm and jerked her around to face him. "Don't you dare laugh at me. Your jealousy seems to rule all of your thoughts and emotions. How did anyone suspect Dwayne of anything?"

"I don't know how, but you can bet that psychic is involved. There's quite a bit of talk around the congregation how she had a vision of Laura Faye when she was interviewing the parents." She yanked her arm from his grip. "I think it's time we take care of her and her little group of followers. It's possible she has psychic abilities."

"If that's the case, then I'll be the one to handle taking care of them."

"Very well, but I'm going to have to be sure Dwayne's taken care of." She watched his fury fade to grief. "We can't afford any more slipups that tie us to these women. I'll alert our flock. We have many chosen on the inside. They'll be sure he never makes it to the interview room."

He slowly turned away from her and walked toward the door. "Yes, he must be taken care of. But I think it's time we finalize our last sacrifice before we go back to the underground, don't you?"

"I agree, wouldn't sacrificing a pesty psychic be very rewarding?" She placed her hand on his arm.

He turned back to her and smiled. "My, my, aren't you quite the anointed one?" He pulled her into his arms and kissed her hard and released her. "Maybe I was too quick to dismiss you and your loyalty. Come. Let us bring bondage to our souls."

She coyly smiled and followed him into the bedroom. "You will always have my loyalty, My Lord."

SEVENTEEN

Jesse paced back and forth in his office and slammed his hand into his desk while yelling at his lieutenant, Joe Greene. "How did this happen? Wasn't anyone watching him? I want to talk to everyone who came in contact with him immediately!"

"Yes, sir, but nobody thought he was a suicidal risk, sir." Joe remained at attention and towered in size over Jesse. "I'll be sure to talk with every one of my men who were in the interview room, as well as lock up."

"You damn well better because he was the best lead we've had in this case." Jesse sat down in his chair and dragged his hands through his hair. "You bring in each officer one at a time into my office. And when we're finished, we'd better come up with some answers, because I find this very suspicious that our first suspect hangs himself just as we were getting close to breaking him."

"Are you getting anything?" Cory softly rubbed Marie's shoulder.

"No, I'm not able to tap into anything here." Marie opened her eyes and looked at Cory. "Are you sure this is the street Jesse said they found Anna Beth?"

"Yeah, this is the exact spot, even though it looks as if they removed the crime scene tape."

Tim took photos with his phone. "Why are you having such a difficult time communicating now, Marie?"

"That's a good question, but I have a suspicion it has to do with our latest pal Demon B. I think he's blocking me. He kept Laura Faye from coming forward and going into the light. I guarantee you he's keeping Anna Beth back as well."

"Oh great, now I feel so much better knowing he's lurking around. Can you see him?" Gale rubbed her arms.

"No, I don't see him, but I can feel him." Marie turned toward Gale. "Do you still have your gris-gris bag on you?"

"Yeah, I'm about ready to hang it around my neck."

"Okay, I just wanted to be sure. I think I may need to put another call into Myra before we meet Jesse at the Bistro. Maybe she can help unlock this block." Marie picked up her purse and hung it on her shoulder.

"Maybe you need to talk with Delia again." Tim continued taking pictures.

"That may not be a bad idea either. I think we need to pull in as many forces as we can." Cory grabbed Marie's hand as they walked toward their hotel. "Speaking of forces, where have your spirit guides been?"

"Yeah, I was wondering the same thing. The last time you saw them was in the interview room." Gale zipped her jacket.

Marie replied, "I'm not sure, but I know they're probably working overtime protecting me. They always come through when I need them. I may have to try and communicate with them, as well. I need to find some way of breaking the block this demon has on me and these women. It's time we put an end to all of this."

They turned the corner from Dauphine Street and proceeded onto Canal Street when Marie spotted a homeless man hunched over hugging his knees. He sat on the ground swaying back and forth, and his eyes were wild as he gave her a sinister smile. Marie couldn't take her eyes off him.

The man waited until Marie was in front of him and then put out his hand for money. "Be careful of where you dwell. They are not what they seem."

Marie stopped and looked at him. "Who is not what they seem, and why should I be careful?"

"The Master is powerful. You cannot destroy him. He will take you with him into the darkness." The man began to laugh hysterically.

Gale whipped around at the laughter. "What was that? Who's laughing? I just heard the most horrible sound of laughter."

Cory stood frozen next to Marie. "Did I just see what I think I saw?"

Tim held onto Gale. "I don't see anything, but I heard the laughter too."

Marie looked at all three of them. "I'm guessing it was a warning. At first, I thought he was trying to help me, but obviously not."

"Okay, I don't see anything. Where did the laughter come from?" Gale put her hands on her hips.

"It was a homeless man, or at least at first, I thought it was." Cory squeezed the bridge of his nose. "I wouldn't have believed it if I hadn't seen him with my own eyes... until he disappeared."

"He disappeared? Are you kidding me? How did Tim and I miss it?"

"You weren't supposed to see him. Only I was, but Cory was right next to me. I'm guessing he wanted to get my attention." Marie shook her head.

"Well, it worked. I have to say that was the scariest thing I've ever seen. I don't know how you deal with it, seeing spirits and demons." Cory held Marie tight in his arms and kissed her forehead. "I do need a drink. Can we stop by the bar at the hotel?"

Marie smiled and dropped her forehead to his chest. "Absolutely, and I believe I'll need one too."

"Make that four. We could all use one. I may not have seen it, but that laugh sure as hell made my legs go numb." Gale grabbed Tim's hand and walked into the hotel.

Marie walked through the door and suddenly smelled decay. "Wow, what is that smell?"

"I know, doesn't it smell good. I think it's coming from the restaurant." Gale smiled and stood next to Tim at the bar.

"No, that's not what I smell; I smell decay or something rotting." Marie stood frozen in the middle of the lobby.

"Decay, why do you smell decay?" Cory stood close to Marie.

"I don't know, but I'm getting that uneasy feeling again. I think it's here."

"What do you mean by it? Do you mean Demon B? Because if you do, I'm not sure if I can handle that again." Gale sauntered over to Marie. "Marie, what do we need to do? Should I get Myra on the phone?"

"That may not be a bad idea, although the smell is beginning to fade." Marie caught her breath and placed her hand on her head. "I think it's making sure we know it's around. Why don't we skip the drinks at the bar and head up to my room? I need to get a hold of Myra immediately."

"I'm calling her now." Gale followed them into the elevator.

Cory grabbed his cell phone. "I think I need to call Jesse. I want to confirm what time we're meeting him at the Bistro, and to fill him in on what just happened."

Gale gave her cell phone to Marie. "Here, Myra wants to Skype us as soon as possible. She wants to make sure you're okay."

Marie grabbed the phone and followed Cory to their room. "Yes, I'm okay. We just had some strange things happen. Can you get a hold of Mimi and have her Skype us? I'll be sure to log on and wait for you. I will, okay, talk to you in a little bit."

Cory hung up his cell phone and plopped down into a chair. "You're never going to believe what just happened. Jesse just told me that Dwayne Lucas hung himself in his cell."

"Oh, man, that's awful. I thought they made sure they got rid of their shoelaces and belts." Tim reopened a bottle of wine and began to pour it into four glasses.

"They do, and they did. But apparently, someone on the inside helped him out. Jesse is interviewing everyone who came in contact with Dwayne." Cory took the wine Tim handed him.

"Isn't he going to be able to meet us later?" Gale sat next to Tim and gulped down her wine.

"Yes, he's still meeting us. He has a lot of information to tell us. Plus, he still has that scarf from the Montgomery girl for Marie."

"Good because it looks as though any answers they would have gotten from Dwayne won't happen now. And if I can get support from Myra and Delia on keeping Demon B out of the way, I may be able to communicate or find out what exactly happened." Marie took a sip of wine.

"Oh, there's your laptop, Mimi's calling you now." Gale sat up and turned the laptop for everyone to see.

"Hello there, thanks for getting together on short notice,

but I needed Myra's help. Who all is there with you?" Marie set her wine glass down and moved closer.

Myra leaned in and smiled. "Hello to you all. Mimi and Harry are with me. Jim had to tend to some business at the store. Marie, I was picking up on some urgent vibrations from you. Is everything okay?"

"Well, as it stands Myra, things aren't so good." Marie filled everyone in on the homeless man in the street, the smell of decay, and Dwayne Lucas committing suicide. "Myra, I can feel the demon's presence. He's been blocking me from picking anything up on these poor women all day. We thought we had a lead with Dwayne in custody, but it looks as though that's gone out the window."

"I see you are wearing the ring I sent you, and that's good dear. Gale, you don't have to wear your gris-gris bag around your neck." Myra chuckled.

"Yeah, I know, but I don't care. I want it front and center." Gale poured another glass of wine. "Just knowing that demon is prowling around has me jumpy."

"I understand Gale but remember what I told Marie, and this goes for all of you, you all need to practice blocking them out of your thoughts. You need to place that brick wall in front of you and place yourself in the middle of a circle of inverted mirrors." Myra's neon pink lipstick clashed with her pale features.

Tim replied, "Oh, that's right. We're supposed to imagine the mirrors facing away from us, right?"

"That's correct, Tim, yes." Myra turned toward Harry. "Harry is going to sit here now and share some information. He'll be able to help you in dealing with this demon."

Harry moved into Myra's seat and pushed his newly taped glasses up his nose. "Hello, everyone, I'm glad to see everyone, but I'm a bit concerned that you're drinking."

"Really, Harry, that's what you're concerned with? And I was beginning to like you." Gale gulped her wine and sneered into the camera of the laptop.

"Gale, please be quiet. He's right. We shouldn't be drinking. It dulls our senses and causes our minds to be easily taken over." Marie grabbed Gale's glass ignoring her shocked stare and moved it to the other side of the table. "Go ahead, Harry. I should have remembered that, but we were a bit shaken up."

"That's okay, Marie, I understand. And all of you have a reason to be shaken up. As we discussed before, for this demon to have appeared to you during the interview, it's apparent this is who this group is worshipping. And I know you realize how powerful this demon is."

"Yes, we do, and I'm pretty sure that was why one of his worker bees appeared as a homeless man a few minutes ago. My concern is this, we're meeting with Jesse in a couple of hours, and he's going to have a scarf from the Montgomery girl for me to see if I can pick up any vibrations." Marie popped a piece of gum into her mouth. "How can I be sure to get something from the scarf and at the same time keep Demon B out of my head or from appearing again?"

Harry wiped his forehead. "I believe you are stronger than you think Marie. For this demon to have sent a messenger in the form of a homeless person is proof that you are protected and are blocking him. You smelled decay in the hotel lobby, so we know he is around, but he's not able to gain access the way he did before."

"Do you think I should contact Delia to possibly do some meditating and form a stronger bond around all of us?"

"Absolutely, I think some added meditating and protection will make you even stronger, especially if you will be weakening yourself through psychometry with the scarf." Harry looked back at Myra and faced the camera again. "Marie, please be very careful when you try the psychometry. Myra and I are very concerned for everyone's safety."

Marie smiled. "We will and having everyone surrounding me has made a difference. My spirit guides popped around when I was dealing with the homeless apparition."

"They did. You didn't tell us that." Gale started to grab the wine bottle and stopped at Marie's stare.

"Yeah, they were there, so I know I'll be fine." Marie looked around at her dear friends in the room. "I want to make sure they're going to be okay. I'm still learning to deal with this myself. I'm not sure if I can protect them too."

Myra came into screen view on the laptop. "Marie, Harry is correct. You are stronger than you think, so don't you have any doubt, dear. This demon will sense this, so throw that thought right out of your mind."

"Thank you, Myra. Right, well, I guess it's time we have a session with Delia and then get on with meeting Jesse at the Bistro." Marie smiled into the camera at the SIPS members. "Thanks again everyone, oh and Mimi, how's Bailey? I miss him."

"He's fine, Marie, and I think he misses you too. He's been moping around the house. He'll be glad to see you when you get back." Mimi gave a schoolmarm look through the camera. "When you all get back."

"Yes, I think we're all ready to come home. Thanks again, everyone, and we'll stay in touch." Marie waved goodbye and logged off the computer.

"Okay, everyone, you heard Harry, no more wine." Marie shook her head at Gale. "You'll get over it. Let's get organized and head over to Delia's. We need to get a lot in place before we meet Jesse."

EIGHTEEN

Tim took a deep breath outside of the voodoo museum. "Okay, that was a new experience for me. The smell of that sage is powerful."

"I know. I got a little dizzy a couple of times." Cory held the door open for Marie and Gale. "But I feel a little lighter now."

Marie stood next to Cory. "Yes, I always do, especially after meditating. Are we ready to help Jesse solve this case?"

Gale fixed the gris-gris bag hanging around her neck. "I am. I'm ready to kick some demon ass."

Marie laughed and shook her head. "Let's not get out of control. I want to avoid seeing this demon altogether."

"I agree with that statement." Tim smiled and grabbed Gale's hand. "Let's go. I'm ready for some more gumbo."

Gale rolled her eyes. "I guess that's going to be the inside joke from now on. Plus, you ate a burger not too long ago."

Cory chuckled and pulled Marie close to him. "Are you sure you're ready to try the psychometry on the scarf? Delia looked a bit concerned when you told her about seeing this demon."

"Yeah, I picked up on that too. But we both believe good far outweighs evil, so yeah, I'm ready to do this. Let's just hope Jesse can still gather more evidence after Dwayne committing suicide."

Tim opened the door for everyone and sniffed at the aroma coming from inside the bistro. "Ah, I think I'll have whatever it is, I smell right now."

"Whoa, I'd have to agree on that one. Man, I can't believe we can't have anything to drink. I need to settle my nerves a little more." Gale pouted as she waited for the hostess.

Marie patted Gale on the shoulder. "You can get something to drink… nonalcoholic."

"Boring, but okay, for this one time only, and because I don't want to meet up with the demon either."

Cory pointed to a back table along the wall. "Hey, there's Jesse. He's sitting at the same place as before."

"He must be a regular." Tim followed everyone over to the table and stared at the patron's food along the way.

Jesse stood up and pulled a chair out for Marie. "How is everyone this evening?"

Gale nodded toward the half-empty bottle of wine. "Apparently, not as good as you are."

Jesse laughed and sat back down. "Well, I've been here for a little while. I needed to unwind after the day I had at the station."

"Yes, Cory shared with us what you told him. I can't believe Dwayne hung himself. Were you able to find anything out?" Marie sat down and placed a napkin on her lap.

"Why don't we give them our orders, and I'll fill you in." Jesse handed his menu to the tall, lean waiter. "I'll have my usual."

Marie held up her hand in response to Jesse, pouring her a glass of wine. "No, thank you, none for me this evening. We're trying to keep our heads clear. It tends to fuzz the brain, and I'm trying to avoid having anyone unwanted slip in there."

Gale pouted and ordered a diet root beer and a burger. "I feel like I'm sixteen again, eating out with my parents. When is the last time I ordered a glass of soda and a burger?"

"Do you even know what soda is?" Tim dodged Gale's punch.

"Okay, I understand. Now that we've ordered, if you don't mind, I'm going to have another glass of wine." Jesse poured the wine and took a sip. "Well, as you know, Dwayne Lucas hung himself by his belt in his cell."

"Isn't it standard operating procedure to remove those items?" Cory took a piece of bread and buttered it.

"Yes, they do, and we did. But someone in the department gave it back to him. My lieutenant and I spent the entire afternoon and part of the evening questioning everyone who came in contact with him. Nobody confessed. So, I reprimanded the entire squad, and no one is allowed to leave the precinct."

Cory's brows went straight up. "The entire squad? You're kidding me? And how did everyone respond to that?"

"I don't care. If the one responsible for giving Dwayne's belt back to him isn't going to come forward, they're all going to suffer. I have my suspicions, but I'm waiting to see if anyone comes forward." Jesse looked at Marie. "But there was some evidence that we found on Dwayne's body."

"What was that?"

"Well, it's a little unpleasant to discuss over dinner, but we found a key." Jesse took another sip of wine.

Gale asked, "A key, what kind of a key? And why would that be unpleasant?"

"We believe it's a mausoleum key, and it was found hidden in a particular area of his body. It wasn't in his mouth."

Gale wrinkled her nose. "Oh, wow, are you kidding me?

They found it in his... you know where? How in the world did it fit?"

Marie shoved Gale's shoulder. "Okay, we get the picture, and I don't think we need any details."

Jesse chuckled. "Without going into those details, this particular key folds like a pocket knife, so it is possible. Now we need to see what mausoleum it unlocks because it was obviously important enough for him to hide."

"Did you think to try the mausoleum where you found..." Cory tried to find the right words. "... your ex-fiancé's sister?"

Jesse gave a half smile. "Yes, I did, and my men are at the cemetery now. It didn't open the same one, but I have them searching the entire cemetery."

"Well, not to change the subject but do you have the scarf with you?" Marie sipped her lemon water.

"Yes, I do." Jesse pulled out a lovely black and gold silk scarf contained in a forensic bag. "Here are some gloves. Although we've run so many tests already, I doubt if it would matter."

Gale grabbed Marie's arm. "Don't you think we should eat something first?"

"Will that matter?"

"Well, I'm just saying, after what happened the last time. I don't know. I guess I'm a little jumpy." Gale grabbed the wine bottle, poured a glass, and gulped it down. "Screw the clear head. I need some reinforcement."

Marie smiled and slipped on the latex gloves. "Go ahead. Your head's usually clearer when you drink."

Gale winked. "Very funny, but true."

Marie took the scarf out of the bag and ran the soft fabric through her hands. "I'm beginning to smell that same odor of decay I smelled earlier."

"I am too. Why do I smell it?" Gale set her glass of wine down and looked at Marie.

"I don't know." Marie closed her eyes and began to place herself in a meditative state. "Okay, Anna Beth is coming forward. She has my spirit guides with her, and a few other guides as well. Anna Beth protected."

Jesse leaned forward. "What else can you see? Can she tell you anything?"

"Yes, I believe the reason she can come forward is that she wasn't indoctrinated into the occult. She was an innocent bystander." Marie's slight smile faded. "Oh, she's crying and wants us to let her parents know she's okay. She has crossed over, but she has been trying to contact me ever since the hotel and cemetery incidents. Wait, I'm feeling blocked a little."

"Blocked from what? Is the demon here?" Gale drank some more wine.

"No, he's trying though, but my guides won't allow it. Okay wait, I'm getting a vision of a struggle. She's struggling, and I see a gag around Anna Beth's mouth. There are faces, but I can't quite make them out. I'm beginning to feel dizzy. This must be when she was drugged."

Cory asked in a soft voice. "Have the faces become any clearer?"

"No, but there are sounds of voices chanting in my ears, and I'm seeing the woman with the snake again. The chanting and drumming are deafening, and Anna Beth is crying louder. Wait a minute. Her eyes are coming into focus. I can see through her eyes, and she's terrified." Marie took a deep breath. "They've laid her on a marble mantle and tied her down. The hooded figures are swooning around her. Torches are being lit, and some of them are carrying them as they circle her."

Cory whispered in Gale's ear. "Make sure you are at the ready. I don't want anything interrupting her again."

Gale nodded and took another sip of wine. "I'm ready, not quite sure for what, but I'm ready."

Marie began to sway. "I hear the music through the drums. Now I hear a gong. It just rang three times. Wait a minute, the chanting has stopped, and Anna Beth is trying to wriggle free. She's screaming louder through the gag, but it's muffled. She sees him. She sees him. He's coming closer, and he's wearing the ram's head, oh and he's naked. Oh, no, no, please don't. Please don't. I'm a virgin."

Jesse leaned over toward Cory. "What is she saying? Is that Marie talking or Anna Beth?"

"I'm pretty sure it's Anna Beth. Marie can feel and see what she's going through."

"He's holding up a cup and speaking in a strange language. He's drinking from it, oh please make him stop. Make him stop." Marie began to cry. "Why are you doing this to her, please stop. Now he's holding a dagger, and he's stabbing her over and over again. Oh, there's blood everywhere. She's not moving. She's dead."

Gale tried to hold back her tears. "Marie, what's happening now?"

"I can see her spirit. Anna Beth's spirit is hovering over her body. She looks so confused, so scared. Wait, she sees him removing the ram's head. Oh no, there he is." Marie grabbed her throat, gasped, and passed out.

Cory quickly kept Marie from falling out of her chair and began to tap her cheeks lightly. "Marie, Marie, wake up. Are you okay? Are you still with us? Oh, baby, please wake up."

Marie opened her eyes and began to struggle. "I've got to help her. We've got to help her."

"Marie, it's okay, it's me, Cory. Gale, Tim, and Jesse are here. You're okay, now." Cory pulled her close to him.

"Oh, Cory, it was horrible. She was so scared. I couldn't

save her. I couldn't stop them." Marie buried her face in his chest and began to sob.

Jesse waved the waiter away. "What do we do? Should we go now?"

Marie quickly picked up her head and held up her hand. "No, no, I'm okay. I need to decompress. It takes me awhile to shake off the feelings she had. I need to see a sketch artist or something. I have his face in my mind's eye. I don't want to lose any of the details."

Jesse got up and pulled out his cell phone. "We can go to the station now. Let me put a call through to have our sketch artist meet us there."

Tim stood up. "But what about our food?"

"Tim, how can you think of food now?" Gale pulled her jacket off the back of the chair and slipped it on.

Cory remained seated next to Marie. "He always thinks of food. You know that. Marie, are you feeling a little stronger?"

Marie smiled and nodded. "Yeah, I am."

"Marie, why are you smiling at the wall?" Gale drank the last of her wine.

"Because my spirit guides are there. They were there the whole time, protecting Anna Beth and me."

Jesse placed his cell phone in his pocket and threw his jacket on. "Right, they're going to meet us in about fifteen minutes. I'll have the waiter get all of our orders together for take-out. Oh, and I may need someone to drive us to the station in my car. The last thing I need is a DUI."

Marie got into Jesse's car and opened the box of food and bit into her crab cake sandwich. "I always get famished after I have a vision like that."

"I need more wine." Gale snagged a few fries from Marie.

Cory put his seat belt on and started the engine. "Which direction is the best way to get to the station?"

"Just flip the lights on Cory. I want to get there as fast as we can and then make a left onto St. Claude Avenue. Follow that until you get to Tulane Avenue. I'll direct you from there."

Tim grabbed the plastic fork and tried to eat his gumbo. "This is a first for me... eating gumbo in a cop car."

"Yeah, you're used to eating in your rescue truck." Gale bit into her burger and sighed. "I am glad we brought our food. I need some substance after drinking that wine."

Jesse looked out the window. "Okay, Cory, take a left onto LaSalle Street and then another left on Perdido Street. The station is on the right. You can pull right in the lot to the left."

Marie waited for Cory to park and began shifting out of the seat toward the door. "I need to get in there soon because I can't lose the details of that face."

"We're almost there." Cory came around and grabbed Marie's hand.

Jesse swiped his ID card and opened the door to the building. "Head straight down the hall and make a right at the end. You'll see my office, go on inside and finish your dinners. I'll be right back with Matt."

Marie followed Tim and Gale and leaned her head on Cory's shoulders. "This has been some wild ride, hasn't it? My adrenalin is pumping full blast."

"I have to say, you held your own on that vision. You didn't let anything take over. I'm proud of you." Cory kissed her cheek.

"Aw, shucks, what can I say?"

Tim turned the light on in Jesse's office and brought in two more chairs. "Wow, I really could use a beer right about now."

Jesse followed them into his office and slowly sat down in his chair. "Marie, I'm going to have Matt come in here shortly, but first, I just received more information from my men at the cemetery. They matched a mausoleum to the key we found."

"Yeah, yeah, don't keep us in suspense. What did they find?" Gale sat forward in her chair.

"They found the remains of what looks like eight or nine bodies." Jesse grabbed his neck and dropped his head back. "They called the CSI division, and they're sifting through to confirm the actual number."

NINETEEN

"You imbecile, didn't I tell you to have those bodies removed?" He slapped the assistant's face and knocked him against the wall. "Because of your incompetence, the police are one step closer to recovering them all. Why didn't you carry out my orders?"

The sniveling man tried to answer. "We did remove a few of the bodies."

"A few, didn't I order you to remove them all?"

She tried to contain her laughter. "Don't you think the blame falls on Dwayne? After all, why was he carrying the key with him? He's the reason the police were able to open the mausoleum."

"It wasn't Dwayne's fault. It was that damn psychic's fault. It's time we gather the congregation for one last sacrifice." He turned toward his second assistant. "Gather everyone immediately. Then, we must ask for guidance from Beelzebub to perform the greatest sacrifice yet."

"It isn't a full moon tonight. If you want this to fall under the order of the moon and please the hierarchy, we must wait until then." She playfully stroked his arm.

"We have no time. It is done. We must go underground immediately. The police will be able to gather the evidence and track us down." He shrugged her hand away. "And you won't be there to help conceal the evidence. Now, let us hurry. We have no time to waste."

CORY SAT THERE in shock and shook his head. "Nine bodies were found, with the possibility of more? Do you need to be there? Should Marie go along as well to see if she can help?"

"No, I can't have any of you involved, remember? She's not even supposed to be here now. But with this latest find, my superiors are a little busy dealing with this to be bothered by anything else." Jesse stood up and walked over to the coffee pot. "Would anyone like a cup?"

"I'll take a cup, please. I need to counter the buzz I'm feeling right now." Gale walked over and took a cup from Jesse. "Don't you think we need to bring in the sketch artist?"

"Oh yeah, I almost forgot about that. I need to get this face down on paper." Marie walked over to the doorway and waved the freckled faced young man into the room.

Jesse stirred three teaspoons of sugar into his coffee and turned toward Matt. "Have a seat in my chair. I need to head down to the morgue and wait for them to begin bringing in the bodies. It's going to be a long night."

Cory stood up. "I'd like to help if I can. I'll be glad to go down with you. Make myself useful."

"Sure, I could use the extra help." Jesse followed Cory out of the office and turned back toward Matt. "Call me the second you finish the drawing. And the rest of you, make yourselves as comfortable as you can."

"Oh sure, it should be easy making ourselves comfortable."

Gale sat down next to Tim. "What are we going to do while everyone else is busy?"

Tim shrugged his shoulders. "I don't know. Just sit here and wait, I guess."

Marie nodded while looking at the sketch pad. "Yeah, that's it. The eyes are perfect, but maybe change the eyebrows a little. The hairline is up a little higher, yeah, I like that."

"Marie, did you see everything in that vision? I mean, did you see all of the details?" Gale shivered and took a sip of coffee.

"Yes, I did. And it was disgusting. My heart is still aching from it. I'm not sure I can get that out of my head. But I can't be distracted at the moment. I need to focus on this face." Marie looked back at the pad. "Yes, that's good... the cheekbones are a little more rounded."

"I hope they catch this maniac and everyone who's involved in all of these murders. What a sad existence for someone to want to be involved in killing these women. What brings people to do such awful things?"

Tim got up and made a cup of coffee. "You heard what Harry said. Many of them have had terrible childhoods and lack self-confidence. They need the feeling of belonging to something... anything. They're usually weak minded and easily controlled."

"Yeah, and their leaders are control freaks." Gale finished her coffee. "I must say, police coffee is awful. I miss my Starbucks."

Marie shot up out of her chair. "That's him... this is the guy in my vision."

Matt sat in silence, stared at the sketch pad, and picked up the phone. "Get me, Commander Irons. Yeah, tell him he needs to see this sketch immediately."

"Why, who is it?" Gale took the pad and stared at the face.

"He looks like an average guy to me. Are you sure this is who you saw? He doesn't look threatening or evil."

"That's who I saw. He's the one with the ram's head."

Cory followed Jesse into his office. "Have you finished already?"

Jesse picked up the sketch pad and looked at Matt and then at Marie. "Marie, are you sure this is who you saw in your vision? This is the man who raped Anna Beth and then stabbed her to death?"

"Yes, yes, this is who I saw. Who is he?"

"Cory, shut the door, please." Jesse sat on the edge of his desk. "Marie if this is who you saw then we have a pretty big problem."

"Why, who is he?" Marie stood behind her chair.

Jesse removed his glasses and rubbed his eyes. "This cannot leave this room. Does everyone understand?"

"Yes, we understand, now will you quit keeping us in suspense and tell us who this creep is?" Gale stood up next to Marie.

Jesse looked at Matt and then back at eight pairs of eyes, staring at him. "This is a sketch of New Orleans First Deputy Mayor and Chief Administrator. He's a right-hand man to the Mayor."

Cory grabbed the sketch pad. "Yeah, I recognize him now. Didn't his department have some issues regarding some illegal use of their vehicles?"

"Yeah, they did. They were using the vehicles for personal use and claiming mileage." Jesse shook his head. "Now the hard part is convincing my superiors to bring him in for questioning. You know how thick blue blood is. I have got to find a way to link him to this case."

Marie sighed. "Then, you believe me?"

"Of course I believe you. The big issue is convincing

everyone else." Jesse looked at his watch. "Look, it's late, and I think you're all going to have to head back to your hotel. This place is going to be crawling with CSI and more detectives than you can shake a stick at. If they see you here, it's going to ball up the works. I can't afford that now."

"I agree, it's almost one in the morning, and we should get some rest." Cory handed Marie her jacket.

"I don't think I could sleep now. My mind is racing. But yeah, we need to get out of here." Marie placed her jacket on her shoulders. "Thanks again for believing me. It's refreshing."

"We're going to keep this picture under wraps for the moment. But it'll come in handy when the timing is right. I'll stay in touch with all of you, and of course, if anything else comes to light, you have my number." Jesse shook Cory's hand. "Watch your back, okay? You still have police protection, but these people are slick. Keep your doors bolted. I'll have one of my men give you a lift back to your hotel."

"I don't know about the rest of you, but I need more wine. This bad tasting coffee has killed my buzz, and I need to get it back." Gale grabbed her jacket and followed everyone out of the office.

"Come on, let's go, shall we?" Marie hooked her arm in her best friend's arm. "And no more wine for you, we're supposed to be keeping our heads clear, remember? If we can't sleep, we can play a game of cards."

"Seriously, you want to play cards? I don't think so. I'm not in the mood for cards. Now, I do have a fun game in mind, but it only involves Tim. So, you and Cory can play cards, okay?" Gale chuckled as they headed out of the police station.

Tim smiled at Cory and shrugged his shoulders. "I have no idea what she means."

Cory sat in the front seat of the police car. "Sure, you don't, buddy. Sure, you don't."

. . .

THE CONGREGATION KNELT before him and repeated the words of worship. The gong chimed three times, and their master raised the chalice and begged for guidance for selecting the chosen sacrifice. The air was thick, and the wind began to howl.

"Beelzebub, we beseech your guidance to give you our last sacrifice. Help us to ordain this lost soul and send her to the bowels of hell. Please guide us in bringing her to your altar and prepare her for your mark. In the name of unholy fellowship, we praise thee." He drank from the chalice and placed it on the altar.

The congregation stood and raised their hands to the sky. She carefully watched their display and smiled at him under her hood. She knew this would be the greatest sacrifice of all, and she couldn't contain her eagerness to destroy the one woman who threatened their very existence finally. For this time, he gave her the consecration to perform the sacrifice, which would set her high among the chosen of the hierarchy.

MARIE TOSSED and turned and tried to remove the images from her mind. The women flew by her in a flash with tearstained faces and bloodstained bodies. She felt a tightening in her chest and smelled the decay hurtle through the air. The white light disappeared, and again, the demon tried to take over her mind. Marie blocked him out of her thoughts and commanded him to leave her presence. But he only laughed and hissed at her and stated she shall soon lose her soul and perish into the darkness. Marie scorned him and pictured a ball of pure white light. The demon became angry when it saw Marie's spirit guides. In a flash, it was gone, but Marie felt more despair and pain and suddenly heard a familiar voice scream for help in her head.

Marie sat straight up in bed and began to cough. "Help her, Cory, help me."

Cory turned on the light and pulled Marie into his chest. "Marie, are you alright? You're soaking wet. What happened? What did you see?"

"I don't know. It was horrible. I think the demon tried to take over my mind again. He said I was going to perish. Oh, and I saw all the faces of the women who were sacrificed flash before me. They were covered in blood." Marie took the glass of water off the nightstand and drank it down. "Then my spirit guides appeared, and he disappeared as fast as he came."

"You're okay. It's alright. You're safe with me. You were strong enough to block him." Cory continued to stroke her hair.

"No, there's something wrong. I still feel this horrible despair. And someone screamed in my head. Someone's in trouble."

Cory jumped at the loud banging on their door. "Who in the world is that?"

Marie sprang out of bed and followed Cory to the door. "It sounds like Tim."

Cory opened the door and almost fell back from Tim's force. "Tim, what's wrong?"

Tim kept his balance and stared at Marie and Cory. "It's Gale. She's gone. I thought she got up to go to the bathroom. When she didn't come back to bed, I called for her. But she didn't answer. So, I went to look for her, and the door bolt was unlatched, and she was nowhere to be found."

Cory grabbed Tim's arm, pulled him into the room, and helped him into a chair. "Okay, sit down, and let's go back over what happened."

Marie stood frozen and felt a chill run up her spine. "They

took her. They took Gail. They have her Cory. Oh, dear God, I can see her, she's screaming, and they have her."

"Who has her? What are you talking about?" Tim flew out of the chair and knocked it over.

"I don't know who they are? But that's who I heard scream in my head. They took Gail instead of me." Marie dropped down into the sofa and buried her face in her hands. "They took my best friend."

Cory grabbed his cell from the counter. "I'm calling Jesse."

TWENTY

GALE FELT THE HARD, damp slab beneath her body. Her head was throbbing, and her eyes felt like lead as she slowly opened them to focus on her surroundings. She realized her hands and feet were tied down to what felt like an altar. The room was dark and musty, and it smelled of mildew and incense. She began to struggle out of her restraints but stopped when she heard a door open to her left.

Gale watched the hooded figure move closer toward her. "Who are you, and what are you going to do with me? My friends are on their way. There is no way you're going to get away with this."

"Would you be quiet? Man, you just don't know when to shut up." Pulling the hood off her head, Brigitte revealed her face. "Do you want them to hear that you're awake?"

"What the hell are you doing here? I knew it. I knew you were some kind of a freak. So, you're involved in killing all of these women? You get a kick out of torturing them?" Gale pulled harder on her restraints.

Brigitte pulled out a knife and laughed at Gales gasp.

"Please, lay still so I can cut these off you. Look, I'm a federal agent, and my name isn't Brigitte Dubois, its agent Dawn McAllister, and I've been undercover with this congregation for the last seven months trying to take down the major players."

"Federal agent, are you serious? Okay, I didn't see that coming. I knew your southern accent wasn't real." Gale sat up and gathered her bearings. "Where the hell are we? It smells horrible in here. Whoa, I'm still a little dizzy."

"We're in the basement of the St. Louis Cathedral on Jackson Square. And yes, it does smell." Dawn handed Gale a pair of jeans and a sweatshirt. "Here put these on. I'm afraid I don't have any six-inch heels for you, but I do have a pair of tennis shoes. We need to get out of here as soon as possible. Once they realize the drugs have worn off, they'll be back. And they have big plans for you."

"Big plans, you mean to tell me they were going to do the same thing to me as they did to those other women?" Gale yanked off the sheer gauze gown and slipped on the clothes. "Clearly, you have no sense of size, these jeans are too short, and the sweatshirt is too big."

"You're kidding, right? You're going to complain about the outfit I just brought you, instead of being grateful that I saved your ass from becoming an offering to the hierarchy?" Dawn helped Gale slowly stand on the ground.

"Sorry, I get cranky when I'm taken hostage and drugged for a ceremonial satanic ritual. So, tell me how the hell are we going to get out of here?"

Dawn pulled out her pistol and slowly opened the door and peered to the left. "Okay, it's clear... oh, and watch your step. I had to get past the guard, and he wasn't very cooperative."

Gale saw the hooded figure slumped over in the corner.

"Yikes, is he dead? Okay, I've seen enough. Where are we going?"

"You don't need to worry about him. Now, let's get moving before anyone else shows up. I need to get you to our safe house on Canal Street."

Gale crouched down against the wall and followed Dawn through a narrow stone hallway. "You know, I'm beginning to remember bits and pieces of things. I remember having a dream. It was wild and thrilling, and I felt like flying."

Dawn turned back at Gale and held her finger up to her lips. "I hear someone at the end of the hall."

Gale remained motionless and leaned her head against the wall and whispered. "I'm still a little dizzy. Just what exactly did they drug me with, and how did they do it?"

Dawn motioned her to continue walking. "I never took part in the drugging process. I was only a part of the congregation, as they call it. I didn't take part in the ceremonies either. It's taken me a while to gain their confidence even to allow me to be involved in this sacrifice, which, according to the master, you weren't the sacrifice they wanted."

"Oh, who was it supposed to be?"

Dawn headed underneath a stairway and opened a small closet-like door. "They were planning on sacrificing Marie, and then they were heading underground, wherever that is."

Gale stopped short and grabbed Dawn's arm. "Marie? They were going to take Marie? Why were they targeting her? I have to call and let her know I'm okay."

Dawn pulled Gale into the doorway and closed it behind them. "First of all, calm down and take this flashlight. You can't call Marie now. I need to get you out of here safely and make my contact. We'll call her when this is over. Secondly, they were pissed at her ability to help the police, unbeknownst to anyone else and the FBI, with leads in the investigation."

Gale flipped on the flashlight and saw a rat run across the stone floor. "Crap, was that a rat?"

"I'm sure it was, and for someone who does ghost investigating, you sure are a wimp in the dark."

"I can deal with ghosts, rats not so much." Gale continued to follow Dawn down the narrow hall. "So, it sounds as if you believe in Marie's ability?"

Dawn turned right and reached an outside door and pointed across the street. "Coast is clear, stay close behind me. My vehicle is the Subaru hatchback in that parking lot across the street."

Gale ran behind Dawn and jumped into the car. "You didn't answer my question."

Dawn rolled her eyes and started the car. "Look, I never doubted Marie's ability. I'm just more of your fact-based kind of gal."

Gale chuckled. "So, I guess André was part of the undercover... no pun intended."

Dawn pulled out of the parking lot and drove through the stop sign. "You really don't know when to shut up, do you?"

"I DON'T CARE how long it takes you, just get it done, and call me as soon as you do." Jesse slammed down the phone and motioned for Marie, Cory, and Tim to come into his office. "Cory, shut the door please and everyone take a seat. I have quite a bit of information for you, and I hope you can tell me more about what happened right before Gale was taken."

Marie wrung her hands, and impatiently sat down. "You've got to find Gale. Jesse, I know they have her. The demon possessed her mind and body and made her walk out of her hotel room. That's when they grabbed her. I know it."

"Okay, okay, you need to relax. I understand you're upset.

Now, what do you mean the demon possessed her and made her walk out of her hotel room. Were you there, did you see this take place?"

"No, I didn't see it, but I saw a vision of it. Let me start from the beginning." Marie took a deep breath.

"Yes, I think that would be best." Jesse took a sip of coffee.

"When we got back to the hotel, we were all still pretty wired. Gale and Tim went back to their room and Cory, and I decided to watch some TV. Eventually, I was able to relax, and we went to bed. But I had a dream about all of the women murdered, and the same demon that possessed me in the interview was trying to come into my dream." Marie took a breath and continued. "I was able to block it, and my spirit guides were there to help. But at the very end, I heard a familiar scream in my head. When I abruptly woke up, that's when we heard Tim banging on our door to tell us Gale was gone. It was her scream that I heard."

Jesse looked at Tim. "Okay, I need to know exactly what happened up to the point you realized Gale was gone."

Tim sheepishly looked at everyone. "Well, as Marie said, we went back to our room... to uh, well, ya know. She drank more wine, and I told her she had had enough. I wanted her to keep her mind clear. She didn't care at that point." Tim looked at Marie. "Sorry about that."

Marie smiled. "It's not your fault. Gale does what she wants to."

"Anyway, after we were... done, we fell asleep. I don't remember anything after that except I heard her get up and I assumed she was going to the bathroom. I guess I fell back to sleep because when I woke up later, she wasn't in bed. When I got up and looked around the hotel room, I saw the bolt unlatched. That's when I realized she was gone, and I went and got Cory and Marie." Tim leaned forward on his knees and dropped his head into his hands.

"Can you remember how much time elapsed from the moment Gale got up, and when you discovered she was gone?" Cory looked at Jesse. "Sorry, reflect reaction."

Jesse shook his head. "Not a problem. I was going to ask the same thing."

Tim shrugged his shoulders. "I don't know. Maybe half an hour or so?"

"Right, well, that certainly gives them enough time to get to where they were going. But where and why is the question." Jesse's office phone rang, and he held up a finger. "Hang on a sec and let me get this. Yeah, this is Commander Irons. Right now, yeah, okay, I'll be right up."

"Did they find Gale?" Marie stared at Jesse.

"No, that was my boss. Apparently, they have some inside information they need to share with me. I'll be right back. Help yourselves to some doughnuts and coffee." Jesse got up and turned back toward Marie. "If there is any way you can do what you do to help us find Gale, that'd be a big help."

"Yeah, I've already thought of that, but I can't seem to clear my mind. I'm too upset."

"Okay, well, I'll be right back." Jesse left his office.

Marie wiped away a tear and looked at Cory. "I can't help her, Cory. My mind is completely blank and fuzzy. I don't understand why. What am I going to do if we don't get to her in time? I'll never forgive myself."

"You can't think like that, okay? Call on your spirit guides. They've helped you and us in the past."

"You're right, I'm creating my own block on them, and I need to clear my thoughts." Marie closed her eyes and began to picture a bright white light.

. . .

"WHAT DO you mean she's gone? Where the hell is she? Who was guarding her?" He slammed his fist onto the arm of the throne, and his eyes bulged out of his head.

"We don't know master. Assistant James was guarding her. He's dead sir." The sub-deacon bowed his head in fear.

"That's it. We must go underground now. We have no time for this last sacrifice. Quickly gather our belongings and meet me at the airport." He looked at her and snarled. "I blame you for this."

"My Lord, we mustn't go now, we are so close. It was my time to make the sacrifice. I will find the psychic this time. I will be sure we have the right woman." She held onto his arm and pleaded.

He pushed her away and motioned to his assistants. "Come, we are leaving. Leave her behind, do whatever you wish. But hurry, we have no time to waste."

She begged for his mercy. "Please, let me come with you. You promised me. I've done everything you asked. You can't toss me aside now. What are they going to do to me?"

His laughter rang throughout the congregation. "Do you need to ask me that? You truly are weak and pitiful. Hurry, get rid of her, and meet me at the airport in an hour."

JESSE WALKED BACK into his office and shoved the papers and coffee cup off his desk. "I can't believe it. I absolutely cannot believe it. I've worked in this department for twenty years, moved up in the ranks, and I thought my peers respected me, as well as my superiors. And then I find out that I wasn't in the loop of this investigation."

Cory picked up the tossed papers and cup from the floor. "What are you talking about? What happened?"

"I was just informed that there had been an ongoing undercover FBI investigation for the last seven months following this congregation. They've had an agent on the inside the entire time."

"You're kidding me? But that could be good news for Gale. If there's an agent on the inside, maybe they can help her?" Marie hopefully looked at Jesse.

"Well, that may be true. But I'm not sure how close the agent was able to get involved or if the agent is close enough to help Gale. But they have a lead on the St. Louis Cathedral. They're sending the SWAT team over, and I'm headed there myself." Jesse threw on a tactical vest and placed his semiautomatic pistol in its security holster. "I'm afraid I'm going to have to ask you all to stay here. They think a sacrifice is about to take place, which means that it could be Gale they're sacrificing. They haven't heard back from the agent yet, so we're moving in."

"Oh, please, don't make me stay back here at the station. You've got to let us go with you. Cory's a police chief. He can be on the scene. Tim and I can stay in the car." Marie walked over to Jesse and placed her hand on his arm. "You have to understand. I feel responsible. I wasn't able to foresee this happening. Please let me come with you... she's my best friend."

Jesse closed his eyes and shook his head. "I shouldn't be saying this, but okay. You can all come, but you have to remain in the car. I'm serious. I can't have any interference. Do you understand?"

Marie smiled and hugged Jesse around his neck. "Yes, we understand. And thank you. Thank you for this."

"Okay, go over and grab a vest in that back room. We're leaving immediately. Meet me out back. I'll have Vinny take you in his car." Jesse stopped Marie in mid-stride. "We're going to find Gale... alive. I promise you that."

Marie stood on her toes and kissed Jesse on the cheek. "I know you will. I didn't expect anything less. Oh hey, you mentioned when we got here, you had some more information to give us."

"Oh yeah, I almost forgot. We pulled Dwayne's cell phone records and found consistent calls made to a couple of numbers. Two of them were track phones and couldn't be traced. But one of them was to Katherine Martin. They went to her studio, and she wasn't there. Isn't she one of the members of BEPS?"

Marie sat in the back seat of the police car and gawked at Jesse. "Yes, she is. You don't think she's involved in these murders, do you?"

"Hard to say, but it looks as though we're soon going to find out." Jesse closed the police car door and pounded on the roof signaling to leave.

EPILOGUE

Marie closed her eyes and slowly filled her lungs and blew out a breath, clearing her mind as she telepathically thanked her spirit guides for their protection. The plane engines accelerated as it began its race down the runway. Gale's giggle made Marie smile wide, giving her the highest satisfaction of friendship and loyalty. And as the plane gracefully lifted off the ground, Marie tried replaying the series of events that took place the night before when all hell broke loose.

There was an odd combination of thrill and fear when they drove in the police car to the St. Louis Cathedral. Marie knew full well there was a chance they would find Gale lying lifeless on a cold slab of marble, covered in blood. Racing against time and approaching a scene of methodical men and women risking their lives to save a complete stranger gave Marie a sense of deep respect for anyone in the emergency service field.

With guns pointing and arms silently waving men and women into the building one at a time, Marie impatiently waited for the outcome. She felt elated to see Gale jump out of a Subaru and run across the street to her in the most hilarious outfit in the world of fashion. Marie laughed hysterically when her best friend fought off FBI agents to allow her passage through the crowd. Realizing her friend was alive created a sense of gratitude, she wasn't sure she could ever express.

After what felt like several hours instead of minutes, the SWAT team led a procession of hooded figures out of the doors of the cathedral in handcuffs. It didn't surprise Marie to see television vans pulling up behind the barricade of police officers. It looked like a scene from one of her favorite cop shows.

But as each congregation member was loaded into the SWAT van, Marie spotted the face of the man from her vision. His eyes appeared more hollow and evil than the sketch she described back at the station. Marie could not fathom how a man in the position as First Deputy Mayor and Chief Administrator could use his power to hurt and destroy so many women and their families. She felt a deep sense of pride when Jesse told her they wouldn't have had the leads to solve this case without her and her unique gift.

Plus, who would have thought Brigitte was an undercover FBI agent. Marie couldn't stop laughing at Gale and Agent McAllister's continued bickering. She knew underneath Gale's hard exterior she was grateful to Dawn, but she would never let anyone know it. Gale finally understood what Delia meant regarding the high priestess card. She had jumped to conclusions about Dawn because she certainly wasn't as she seemed.

The most shocking revelation was learning that the person in the body bag being wheeled out on a gurney was Katherine Martin. They were told she was next in line with their hierarchy of the congregation. She had been found in one of the lower small chapels hanging naked upside down on a cross... skinned and disemboweled. Marie couldn't stop thinking of how that could have been Gale. They all privately kept that thought to their selves.

Jesse showed them the list of members. There were police officers, medical examiners, the chief forensic pathologist, grocery clerks, priests, gas station owners, a judge, and the list went on and on. It made sense why Jesse's case files never matched up to the forensic results because of the occult members on the inside contaminating evidence.

They learned this alliance had been established as far back as the seventies. The weakest members of the group told them of murders that spanned over forty years and of the new bodies still lying in mausoleums all over the French Quarter.

The one regret Marie had was not being able to help Laura Faye cross over to the other side. Her guides explained that she was still being held back by Demon B and that it would take stronger forces to cross her over into the light. Before Marie could take on this endeavor, she would need to learn more about her ability and herself.

Drifting back to the present, Marie heard the airline captain tell them they were at thirty-two thousand feet and would be landing at Charleston International Airport in two hours and forty minutes. She was glad to be going home. She missed Bailey, the clinic, and of course the SIPS team. They had informed her there were numerous calls to return for possible investigations. She was pleased with how far they had come in the last six months.

Suddenly Marie felt an eerie wave of nausea and smelled a quick odor of decay. She tried to block it, but she knew who was invading her psyche. Instantly she heard, you cannot escape... you will soon succumb to me.

Cory grabbed Marie's hand. "Are you okay? You practically jumped out of your seat."

"No, no, I'm fine. I'm ready to go home." Marie smiled and kissed Cory's cheek.

She leaned her head back and realized a portal was open. One she wasn't sure she could close. Knowing this was a new area of the unknown, she felt it best to get answers from Myra and her spirit guides. It was time she learned to block Demon B permanently.

Dear reader,

We hope you enjoyed reading *Secret of the Big Easy*. Please take a moment to leave a review, even if it's a short one. Your opinion is important to us.

The story continues in *Federal City's Secret*.

Discover more books by Robin Murphy at https://www.nextchapter.pub/authors/robin-murphy

Want to know when one of our books is free or discounted? Join the newsletter at http://eepurl.com/bqqB3H

Best regards,
Robin Murphy and the Next Chapter Team

ABOUT THE AUTHOR

Robin Murphy has worked in the administrative, graphic design, desktop publishing, writing, and self-publishing realm for more than thirty-five years. Her wide range of skills and abilities place her at the top of her field.

The second book in her paranormal mystery series is *Secret of the Big Easy*, the third is *Federal City's Secret*, the fourth is *Secret of Coffin Island*, and the fifth is *Savannah's Secret*. She is also a freelance and travel writer.

Robin has been a speaker on author platforms, self-publishing, and marketing. She has also written *A Complete "How To" Guide for Rookie Writers*, which is a very practical, hands-on and user-friendly book to enable a rookie writer to learn how to get their newly created work produced and available to readers, as well as, a comedic romance titled, *Point and Shoot for Your Life*, which was a ReadFree.Ly 2016 Best Indie Book Finalist.

You can find Robin's books on her Amazon author page.

ALSO BY ROBIN MURPHY

Marie Bartek and the SIPS Team Series:

Sullivan's Secret

Secret of the Big Easy

Federal City's Secret

Secret of Coffin Island

Savannah's Secret

A Complete How-To Guide For Rookie Writers

Point and Shoot for Your Life

Secret Of The Big Easy
ISBN: 978-4-86747-425-9

Published by
Next Chapter
1-60-20 Minami-Otsuka
170-0005 Toshima-Ku, Tokyo
+818035793528

20th May 2021

Lightning Source UK Ltd.
Milton Keynes UK
UKHW012058030621
384904UK00001B/203